Living as a Mistake

by

Amy Ondriezek

PublishAmerica
Baltimore

© 2008 by Amy Ondriezek.
All rights reserved. No part of this book may be reproduced, stored in a retrieval system or transmitted in any form or by any means without the prior written permission of the publishers, except by a reviewer who may quote brief passages in a review to be printed in a newspaper, magazine or journal.

First printing

All characters in this book are fictitious, and any resemblance to real persons, living or dead, is coincidental.

ISBN: 1-60474-866-4
PUBLISHED BY PUBLISHAMERICA, LLLP
www.publishamerica.com
Baltimore

Printed in the United States of America

Dedication

I am dedicating this book to those who have supported me no matter what I went through in my life. I mean it when I say this is for my Pappy, because he was the man that every man should want to be like. I do remember him; all the good things, and those are the qualities I have always wanted to find in any man I met, whether he became a friend or more. My Pappy has always been the main man in my life, and I've always wanted to have the unique qualities that he had that made us all love him so much.

I want to thank PublishAmerica for giving me the opportunity I had always dreamed of, and I hope they continue to have the support in me that they have had from the day they read my work.

I could never forget to thank Jackie, who has been my sister since the day I met her. We are intertwined with each other and nothing can change that, and nothing ever will.

And I can't forget my Aunt Jeanne, my Grammy, Dave, Ralph, Jessy G, and my little man, Connor. They are my support system that has never changed throughout my life, and has always been there, and been strong, no matter how bad my day was.

There are two people left that I truly want to thank for supporting me and loving me no matter what happened in my life. They are my mother, Harriet, and my husband, Allan. Mom, from the day I was born, you began teaching me how to live my life, shape my morals and my values, and to live life as if each day were my last, and not to leave anyone in anger or hurt. You are truly my hero, Mom. I also wanted to thank you for the people you have allowed our family to help shape us into. When we truly needed love and support, they were always there for us, and you never turned them away, making them develop into so much more than "just" uncles, "just" aunts, etc. We are ONE, and there is no such thing as extended family. And Allan, baby, since the day I met you, you have always told me I could do whatever I put my mind to, and now, in every page after this one, I have accomplished what I dreamed of. Thank you for always standing beside me, never behind me or in front of me, and for always pushing me when I needed it and supporting me when I deserved it. You are the best thing that has ever come into my life.

Prologue

Kerry is aiming to be a better person in her life, and attempting not to become her mother. She has to recognize her biological father as the evil cretin he is, instead of waiting and wondering when he will come to love her.

I personally hope that Kerry's life affects someone out there, and that they take into account how she had to change, learn from her mistakes, and become a better person than she had expected to become. I hope that someone can be inspired enough by her story to have their hope restored and to give more love than they care to receive. I want one person to understand and one person to be happier, knowing that the old saying actually is true…"The best is yet to come."

And It Begins...

Kerry decided young that love was a non-existent concept and that there was nothing good about it. She had been hurt enough times on a "wow, love at first sight" basis that she had totally given up on the concept of finding her one true love. As a little girl, she was raised in a single parent home. That fact led to her having pretend fantasies not including a father figure. She used to pretend that she was the funniest, happiest (pretend) mom that raised her (pretend) children all by herself, without anyone's help. As she got older and understood what her mother went through on a daily basis, she prayed every night that she would not end up alone.

The first person to hurt her the deepest and to leave the most permanent scars was the one person she was raised to believe she should love and trust forever. To believe that she *could* love and trust forever. That man was her biological father. She met him when she was a mere seven years old. It was such a happy day because she didn't have a father figure at all until then. She was being shown what she had been missing for all those years. He gave her so many hopes and so many dreams, telling her that so many things were going to change. He did not lie about that, but to a seven-year-old, Kerry did not ever expect to find out her own father lied to her more often than he saw her. That's pretty bad. That day though, Kerry's new world was lightened up, ever so briefly. She could see that everything was going to change, not nearly just what he had mentioned. She found out that he was already married and she was no longer an only child. It only took her a few years to figure out how long he had been married, and that it was more years than her age. Kerry should have realized then that if he couldn't be honest in his own marriage and to the one person he promised his love and companionship to forever, he couldn't be honest to her, his mistake. Nevertheless, she was now the youngest of three children. Unfortunately, she also discovered she was unwanted greatly by her new brother, her new sister, and by her father's wife. She despised Kerry's existence with a great passion that she could not understand at only seven years old. He promised Kerry so much when she was so young and innocent that day. Maybe he thought she would forget as she got older. She didn't, but she did grow more bitter.

1

Let's backtrack a little and give a bit of background information before Kerry's story begins to unfold and she discloses how her father inadvertently tried to ruin her life, and how she then tried to pick up the broken pieces.

Kerry was raised by her mother, Angelica; grandmother, Dot; two uncles, Wesley and Paul; an aunt, Janine; and her grandfather. Her grandfather, Wesley, Sr., was her hero. She looked up to him for everything, and that wasn't only because she was a short three-year-old. However, as Kerry came to learn, good things never last and always go away too soon, and he passed away on March 18, 1986. A huge part of her died with him. It was a part of herself that led her to become very untrusting and unloving to new people. She called him her "pappy," but he assumed the role of "daddy" because of her lack of a biological father figure. He was her daddy because he was the only one there to fill that spot. Her whole life changed when he passed away, as well as the lives of the rest of her family. They had all looked to him for all the answers, and all of a sudden, the answers weren't coming. He was the glue in the family, and now they suddenly needed to look to each other for the answers, which would be a huge change. Pappy died exactly one month before Kerry turned four, but her memory of the night before he died is vivid, as if it was yesterday. The memories haunted her for her entire life, because she shouldn't be able to remember them. She was so little, and it was so long ago. The things she didn't remember, she was told through family stories. For example, for her cousin's first birthday, he left to get her something, but came back with a gift for Kerry as well as her gift. Kerry kept that teddy bear he got her that day, and although the thing has been through thick and thin, it is still around. Kerry believes it brings her good luck. Kerry does still remember the night before he died though. Tears prickle her eyes just thinking about him, wishing she could go back for only one hour to make the most of his last evening. She would trade everything just to be able to tell him one last time how much his life influences everything she says or does. That night though, she ran to him, climbed onto his lap with crayons and coloring book, and they picked out a picture and colored it together. That's the last thing she would ever do with him.

    In the hospital, Kerry still wasn't old enough to be in the room with him, so she had to stay out in the waiting room with a family member, but her memory reflects seeing the bottom half of his hospital bed, only the bottom half though. Remembering the cold plastic chair positioned exactly opposite of his room. Raising her head ever so slowly, tears flowing down her chubby cheeks. The top half of his bed was covered with all those helpful machines that were working to help Pappy through his heart attack. The entire family was all standing at the foot of his bed, crying, and Kerry was crying too because she was denied entrance to his room. Strange though, because the waiting room was nowhere near the room, and there's no way Kerry could have seen this. It had to be a dream, but it's strange that it has stayed with her for so long. The doctors told her family he would pull through, most likely with a full recovery, but he didn't. Because of the incompetence and arrogance of those doctors, Kerry's heart broke for the first time, and she began to understand then that she would have to learn how to be strong.

    She wasn't allowed at the funeral, but her mother took her to the viewing for one last time to see him. As Kerry walked up to the casket, a path was being made by the guests. Kerry's mother, Angelica, and Kerry gave him a red rose and kissed him good-bye, forever. Her innocence nearly broken, she looked up at her mother with unknowing eyes and asked why Pappy was so cold. Angelica held back tears desperately, but she just smiled at Kerry and said she knew. Not exactly an answer to Kerry, but when she said that, Kerry's tears began to flow, knowing she would never see her beloved Pappy ever again, but not quite understanding why.

As for friends, Kerry's mother had been best friends with Hannah for many years, and they got pregnant around the same time, one month apart. Therefore, when the kids were born, Mark and Kerry were immediately labeled best friends. They were forced onto each other from the beginning, and no matter what happened in their lives, they had to make up, because they were "best friends." Hannah and Angelica said so. They didn't grow apart for many years, and then it did mend itself on its own, but those years apart were hell, at least for Kerry. Mark didn't have his father in his life either, but he tried to buy Mark off with gifts instead of time spent together. His parents had just divorced, and his mother remarried. He became very rebellious and did not get along very well with his stepdad, and by then his mother as well, but that is a different story. As for his real father, though, that is one deep connection that helped his friendship with Kerry last a long time. Similar haunts ran through their minds as to whether their fathers loved them or not. His father tried to win him over with buying him things, and Kerry's didn't seem to mind using lies to try to win her over, if he was in fact even trying to win her over at all.

2

    Before the true father comes around, another death bruises Kerry's young heart. Her tearful aunt came into her bedroom and woke a little ten-year-old Kerry up. Before she could even ask, Kerry began crying, because her aunt was crying. She said Mark's grandma passed away. Emma was the highlight of Sunday mornings. For small children (and actually some adults too), church is not exactly the greatest part of the week. Emma would brighten up Sunday morning just by being there. Kerry loved her; she was another grandmother to her. Never to replace the original, but it is always good to have as many family members as possible. Emma would just swallow you in her hugs because she was a big woman, and Kerry and Mark were just tiny children. Kerry would always feel so safe and secure when she would hug her that she never wanted her to let go.
    One Sunday morning, Mark and Kerry were sitting beside the very religious Emma, when Mark gave her a lollipop. They were licking away, pretending to listen to the preacher do his thing, when all of a sudden they heard this big echoing gasp and their lollipops were snatched out of their hands mid-lick. Emma's eyes were wide, and it was all the children could do not to laugh at her, when she tried to lecture them about eating during his sermon.
    Then there was a punch in the gut by a strong imaginary fist when she was diagnosed with breast cancer. Kerry can still remember the last time she saw her. She was calling Kerry and Mark "sweetie," but only because the cancer made her forget their real names and how much they loved her. Kerry knew it wasn't her fault she couldn't say hi to them, but it hurt her anyway, as she was sure it did Mark. She

passed away shortly after. That was one of the first times Kerry realized that she was better at helping and handling other's problems, rather than facing her own head-on.

3

    Then Calvin came into the picture. Kerry was seven years old, and the only father figure she ever had was her Pappy, and he had been gone for a few years now. She still had her two uncles, but they weren't the type to be the missing father figure. They were awesome uncles, but they were always more like friends or brothers than a father. And Kerry would never want to compare them to her biological father anyway. Anyway, Kerry was at her grandmother's house, and she looked out the window and saw a strange man at her house, talking to her mother. Curious, Kerry stepped outside to ask her mother who it was, and she asked if Kerry would like to meet her father. Excited at this prospect, she readily agreed (being only seven), and her mother said, "Well, here he is."
    He was not what Kerry had expected. When you don't have a father, you imagine him to be the greatest looking guy who has a hug-me kind of persona. Kerry expected him to be warm and open as she remembered her Pappy to be. This person standing groggily in front of her was somewhat scary, and she did not want to hug him at all. He had black hair, going gray and a little bald, and he was rather tall. Kerry could smell the liquor on his breath, and she wondered why he would drink prior to this meeting. He sat down with Kerry and talked though, and told her about his "other family." This "other family" was not quite what Kerry expected at all. She wanted someone to call her "sis," and someone to hug her and say they were so glad they had finally met her. That is *not* what she got. She quickly found out that he had a brother, and that he lived only an hour away. Kerry also learned that her neighbor, whom she called Uncle Danny, was actually her real uncle.

This was the best news, because he seemed like family already. And his daughter, whom she played with every day, was actually her cousin. Her father promised her many things though, and she believed him. Why shouldn't she have? Upon meeting him for the first time, Kerry had a lot high expectations of him. Those standards dropped drastically when she got to know him a little, and now she expects nothing of him. He meets that expectation, and that one alone.

When Kerry met her brother, it was a one-time occasion. His black hair was short and crew-cut, and he was tall and lanky. His brown eyes were almost black, and they looked like something out of a horror flick, and were very troubling, even though he was very nice to Kerry, and even played with her. She was eight then, and her brother had come up for Christmas with his at-the-time boyfriend. This was new to Kerry, because she had never dealt with any kind of homosexuality in her life before, but she came to understand his boyfriends changed as quickly as the days of the week. Nevertheless, Kerry liked Joe, because he introduced her to his boyfriend as his little sister. He gave off a nice impression then, but he never saw Kerry again, and his mother instilled it into his head that Kerry was to be hated. He obeyed his mother. Two years later, Joe called Kerry's house, and although her mother had already answered it, Kerry picked up another receiver. The words she heard tore her up inside. Kerry heard Joe's voice, but it was no longer sweet and kind, as it was when he had spoken to an innocent eight-year-old. It was cold and heartless as his eyes had been as he swore and cursed Angelica's name, and all Kerry could do was picture his eyes getting blacker as the words pierced through her ears. The cold, heartless eyes that didn't seem to have any caring depth to them. He said that no matter what proof Angelica could come up with, Kerry would never be considered his sister. No matter what happened, Kerry would never be related to him. He reiterated that Kerry would remain an only child forever. She would never even have a half-sister and half-brother. She remained silent as she listened to Joe bad-mouth her. The hurt filled Kerry's mind, and she was lost as to what to do about it. She did not understand what she had done to deserve this. She never even asked to meet Calvin or any of his real family. She had asked who he was, but never to meet him and ruin people's lives. Kerry hung up the telephone as quietly as possible; she did not want her mother to know she had heard what Joe said. Later that evening, Kerry called Mark, and hid in the back bedroom so her mother would not hear the tearful confession. Mark was the only person Kerry believed she could trust, and she did not know her mother could still hear her tears, but she knew she couldn't have been any quieter. She also had no idea at the time that she wasn't a burden to Angelica. She often felt that way, especially after hearing the awful things Joe said about her. She felt it was all her fault. How could she have ruined her mother's life like that? If she had only known at the time; her mother was her was everything, and they could have been holding each other, not hiding from each other.

Kerry's "sister" avoided any type of contact with her or Angelica. It seemed that she knew of all the drama surrounding poor, young Kerry, and wanted nothing to do with it. Kerry was more than relieved to have nothing said to her than a repeat of Joe's phone call. Kerry did end up meeting her, though, and her daughter. Kerry's neighbor's daughter was celebrating a birthday, and her mother was very good friends with Kerry's "sister." Shannon showed up, and her daughter played with Kerry, never realizing she was playing with her aunt. Kerry watched the little girl's actions and tried to see if she was anything like her. Kerry was relieved to come to the conclusion that she was only like her mother. Having seen so little of her father, though, she couldn't really tell if any of his genes were evident in her behavior. But at least Shannon was civil to her and allowed her to interact with the only niece Kerry would ever have, and yet never see again.

4

A few years went by the same, barely speaking to each other, worrying somebody might see them in public then he would have to explain it to his wife. Kerry and Calvin almost never saw each other, and he called when he was at work (he was hired at as an accountant close to his new house). Kerry did not even know his home number. Every time she had to fill out a piece of paper for school that asked for phone numbers of parents, and work numbers for parents, tears threatened to break loose. It was not fair having such a different background than everyone else. Most of the time when parents are separated, they at least let the child live happily. Kerry felt she was carrying burdens from both parents, and it killed her that her non-sister and non-brother hated her so badly without even knowing anything about her, or attempting to know anything about her. She had his blood, nothing else, and she was to be despised because of it. She was in her teens now, still hating him so badly. She pretended to love him for her mother, but her heart was stone to him. She rarely called him at work, because he would often not come to the phone anyway. And if she had to call for some reason, if only to appease her mother, she always asked for "Dad"… just to piss him off. And it always did. Isn't that sad how someone can get into trouble for that? Most parents expect it and ground children who try to be adults.

Angelica became Kerry's rock through her life. She did have friends, and one best friend, but hid everything. But if she did need to vent, her mom was always there. Even if she couldn't bring herself to actually talk about the problem, she could go lay her head in her mom's lap and just be held, or receive a backrub. This was her safe-haven, and she often lay there with her. If anyone had a shitty life or a shitty biological father, Kerry always prayed they had someone like her mother.

5

When Calvin moved from being an hour away to a few miles away, he promised things would change. One could only hope things would change. He was still a raging alcoholic, still fighting with his wife, and still using Angelica only when he "needed" somebody to believe in him. During one argument with his wife, he ended up leaving, but upon his arrival back home, drunk of course, instead of parking his car, he simply drove it through the garage, door down and everything. Kerry was embarrassed to be kin to someone like that, but the one good thing about him was that nobody really knew he was kin to her. At his new home, though, he opened his own accounting firm (which shortly turned into his own bankrupt accounting firm), and promised he would make more time for Kerry. She visited him once while he lived there. The only times he ever visited were at Christmas and on her birthday, which he was usually reminded of because of Angelica.

No Matter What...
He calls, when he remembers.
That's not often, but at least he knows my number.
I consider myself lucky, he knows my name.
He drinks too much, and makes bad decisions.
But I'll always love him, and nothing can change that.
I've known him too long, and can't change the way he is.
I like his forgetfulness, his worry, and his complaints.
I like the way he makes excuses, and the way they are always corny.
I know, deep down, that he loves me too.

But he doesn't know how to show it, and can't learn how.
But we love each other, and we both know it.
We will be attached for life, and there's nothing either one of us can do about it.
No matter what anybody says and no matter what you do, I'll always stick up for you.
I'll stand by your side, and always say nice things about you.
I like your lies, and the fact that they reoccur.
There's nothing about you I would change, except for her.
That other woman, the one who prevents you from sharing your love.
Mom and I accept this, and we will live our lives every day dealing with your absence.
But, Dad, I will always love your quirky behavior, and I don't want to lose it.
So, no matter what she says, please love me, and don't forget I am around.

Kerry starting sneaking a lot of drinks from Angelica's liquor cabinet. Kerry used to lie awake dreaming of a simple life, one that included a three-person family—Mom, Dad, and little Kerry—and they'd have family vacations, birthdays with lots of laughter, giggling at her if she didn't blow out all the candles, and a Mom and Dad who kissed while Kerry and her friends went "Eww!!!" in the background. It took her only a short while to realize she never dreamed of that for herself, but for her mom. She admired her mother so much, she always wanted to grow up just like her, and she figured that if her mother ended up with a fairy-tale ending, then Kerry would have that much more to look forward to, instead of the single-parent lifestyle her mother was now living.

6

Because of all the things that Calvin said and didn't do, and all the losses Kerry felt she was facing, her faith in God had lapsed slightly. She had always thought if she prayed hard enough, God would fix whatever was wrong with her mom, whether it be to have an easy day at work or a week without a drunken phone call from that asshole who thought he was her father. It seemed that her prayers were going unanswered lately, and she was at a loss as to what to do, other than believe He didn't care and wasn't going to help. And when her Aunt Ruth died, Kerry's faith almost went along with her. She cried for almost an hour, and school the next day was awful. The night after the funeral, she cried before her sleep, again. This time, she prayed for a sign, and for reassurance. Aunt Ruth was one of the most innocent people Kerry knew; she was everything anyone should want to be like. The most giving, sensitive, sweetest woman you could meet. And to see her taken away was the worst feeling in the world. But Kerry prayed hard, wanting a sign Aunt Ruth was okay, and happy wherever she may be. She felt she could never sleep with the horror-filled images of her aunt wandering aimlessly around with nowhere to call home, and nobody to protect her. Loving the cleansing feeling of rain, that is exactly what Kerry prayed for, which seemed to be a long shot in a summer with a horrible dry heat, but she figured if she needed proof that badly, God could pull off a miracle. She swore her faith would return if it just rained, just a little bit, sometime tomorrow.

Saying Goodbye
I went to the store and got some new dress clothes.
I just had to look decent to see Aunt Ruth's heavenly pose.
When I saw her, tears sprang to my eyes.
It's so hard to let go, to say your good-byes.
Even harder when they are one-sided.
The disappointment, it's so hard to hide it.
The wind whipped around our hair
As we gathered on the hill to show we care.
Somewhere they was joy, maybe a mother giving birth,
But the tears flowed as we lowered my aunt into the earth.

Kerry had volunteer work the next day for a festival put on by her school. She was frozen all day but managed to stay cheery to all the children while everyone else complained about the weather. Soaked to the bone by noon, but loving it, she danced in it with the children. She felt God had given her something more than anyone could have ever received, and she was going to appreciate it. That night, Kerry got down on her knees beside her bed and thanked God for all the gifts He gives, that maybe we do not see all the time. She came to a true understanding that day about her faith.

Our Angel's Smile
Thinking about that laugh, always full of joy and happiness.
It's easy to see how quickly the time has passed.
Her smile was actually contagious, we couldn't be near without it taking us.
Always to the same place, and to where she went now.
We can't join her this time, she's flying solo.
We can only gather here crying, wanting to go.
She's our angel now, hovering near.
A song plays, do you hear?
Her song lifts her up, up, her smile is for all now.
Not just for the family, but for God, so for Him our angel takes her bow.

7

He wasn't the worst father, but he wasn't far from it either. The memories Kerry had of him, she would pay damn good money to get rid of. The worst ones were when he would call drunk though, and that was quite often. One night, when she was fourteen, it was around nine, and he called, completely wasted, already. He told Angelica to meet him at the old cemetery near where he used to work (no public places, they could never be seen together), but he specifically requested for Kerry's appearance. She was really mad at her mom for saying she would be there; she hated him drunk because he scared her. Her mother said she had to go though, because she never got to see him, and she should take every opportunity she got. When they got to the back of the cemetery, where they stored the backhoes and lawnmowers, he put country on the radio in Angelica's car and was dancing drunkenly around the car. Kerry was being rude to him, and after receiving repeated dirty looks from her mother, she finally stopped and went dead silent. Her father had decided he was thirsty, and told Angelica to run to the nearest gas station to get some sodas for all of them. She ran over to the door, eager to leave for any reason, but he said, "No, not you, you can stay with your daddy." Kerry rolled her eyes, but returned to his "dance floor." He turned the radio on in his car, and a slow song came on. In a drunken stupor, he tried to dance with Kerry without falling over. His movements got slower and slower, and his head bobbed towards Kerry's shoulder. She really thought he was going to pass out on her, and she was worried about how she was going to hold his fat ass up. But then he started talking. Nonsense words that turned into plain old babble that didn't even make sentences. The only words Kerry got were him saying he loved her and she was such a good girl. His hands lowered then and they were on Kerry's hips, not her shoulders. His trap stopped talking and started kissing. Her cheeks, her forehead, and finally her lips. They lingered, and she pursed her mouth shut and closed her eyes, ready to cry. She trembled in fear, and prayed for her mother's quick return. The slow song had ended, so that had not helped. She did not even want a soda now, and she doubted her biological father's thirst as well. He started trying to French kiss Kerry, and she almost started crying then. Like she wanted her first French kiss to be with her biological father. Disgusting. She tried to back away only to realize that she was up against his car. She realized also that his hands were on her butt, and trying to get into her pants. She squeezed her eyes shut and tried to concentrate on the song on the radio, her lips still pursed shut as tightly as she could get them. A few stray tears escaped out of her eyes as her father attempted to push her up against one of the graves. He was trying to pull her hands away from her protective stance of them pressing her pants into her legs, when her mother's headlights suddenly appeared. Calvin saw them first (Kerry's eyes were still clamped shut), and he backed away quickly, almost falling over a small grave. Kerry ran to her mom's car, wiping her eyes, looking at the ground. She got out, handed Kerry a soda, and asked what was wrong. She mumbled that the headlights were too bright, grabbed her soda, and got in the car. She followed Kerry, repeating her question, but she just said she was really tired. She locked all the doors except the driver's door, and waited impatiently to go home. She was still scared, and she really wanted to take a shower. She felt so nasty and dirty, and she just wanted to sit there and cry, but she did not want to tell her mother. She figured it would take a few days to wash off all his nasty ass germs, which were all over Kerry's suddenly disgusting body. She had never hated her body, but she did now. It had betrayed her by becoming a target that she had seen on after-school specials and late-night movies. She did not want to be that kind of person or end up like those people did, taking bottles of medications and crying to their therapist (who was also their best friend). It seemed to take forever for Calvin to chase Angelica around random graves trying to get her to have sex with him in the graveyard, but finally Angelica told him to get away and that she had to get Kerry home to finish her homework. Calvin tried to give Kerry a hug, but she waved through the window instead, still not smiling. Her mother gave her "the look" that mothers have though, so she got out and let him hug her, holding her butt out so he wouldn't be tempted to grab it. He said he loved her, his stinking breath all over Kerry's distressed face. She hated him more than anything and she hoped he would never call her again.

On the way home, her mom kept asking her what was wrong, but she just kept saying repeatedly that she was tired. She finally stopped asking. At home, she went straight into the shower and cried into the scalding hot water. When she got out, she was wrinkly and as red as a lobster. She hoped she did not have burns, but she felt a little cleaner. She knew she would shower again in the morning though, in case his germs came back in her sleep.

Kerry hid this incident for almost nine years. When her mom finally found out about the "dancing" incident, she was not very thrilled about it. But you cannot help who you love, or so Kerry had heard.

8

Around this time, Calvin was arrested for beating up his wife, Acacia, outside a bar. Kerry found out from him (although she assumed he was lying) that he pulled Acacia's hair and threatened, "You wait until you get home." Acacia was sporting fresh new sunglasses and carrying her arm tenderly, hiding the fact that it was in a sling. Allegedly the patrons of the bar were the ones who called the police. According to her, she wasn't afraid of him, but the other drunks at the bar must have been afraid for her. Kerry felt the whole situation was stupid. She didn't agree with men who hit women, but she also didn't believe this was the first time, so she thought it was coming to her.

Calvin immediately called Angelica with his one phone call, asking for money. Sadly enough, within a few hours, Kerry and Angelica were another $600 in debt. He claimed he needed $200 for his bail and another $400 to leave the state. Her poor mother, way too giving, and he couldn't just leave them alone. If he did not show up to court, Angelica was told she might have to pay as much as $2,000. That is, if Acacia showed up and Calvin didn't. They couldn't afford groceries, and he knew this, but he just swooped on in, to take and take and take, then just leave them, as if they were nothing. That's what they were to him. A big fat nothing. It seemed perfect for Calvin to be the kind of man to hide from his problems, like as if he leaves the state, they will magically disappear. He would never have been a wife-beater or an attempted child molester. He constantly, conveniently forgets his accidents and mistakes, and his wimpy ass didn't even have the balls to ask Angelica if he had done anything to Kerry or not. Then

LIVING AS A MISTAKE

again he denied beating Acacia, so why would he admit or even ask about touching Kerry inappropriately? Even thinking of him made Kerry take another hot shower, not a bath; bathing would make the germs fester in her pores.

While on his vacation from reality with his for-real son in Montana, he said that Angelica and Kerry could write to him at his new job, selling jewelry in a local mall. They could not call though, and if he called them, it was collect, so Joe would not know whom he was calling. The letters even had to go to his work; he did not want Joe to get them. Not that Kerry wanted to write to him anyway, but Angelica made her, and it was boring "how are you" stuff. The juicy letter was Angelica's, and she sent it riddled with "I miss you's" and "I love you's." They sent only those two letters. He only got one. And from my non-brother's response, you can guess which one he got.

Joe wrote back:

> *Even if that little bitch is my father's daughter, I will never consider her to be even my half-sister. You and she are never going to be even the same class as my family is, and it's all because you screwed my father.*
>
> *Do you really think my father only screwed you besides my mother? I'm sure there are other inbred children out there because he blew off his vows! Do you realize how many whores he has slept with who might have had children, but they never bothered us! In absolutely no way should you even be bothering my sister, my mother, or my dad because you had to get your rocks off.*

Angelica never received that letter. Kerry got to it first, and it affected her deeply. She was hurt deeply simply because Joe had called her mother a whore. Her mother had only ever slept with two people! Joe probably slept with two people just last night! Anyway, she wrote back to her non-brother, and planned to hide these episodes from her mother. The only problem was that Joe wrote back to her, and it had to arrive on her mother's day off. She actually got drunk after she read it, and around one in the afternoon, she picked Kerry up from school, drunk. This letter scarred Angelica, but it didn't hurt Kerry because it was to her, not her mom. She can handle stabs at herself, because she wasn't exactly popular in school, so she'd been living with ridicule her entire life, making getting it from a twenty-something with nothing better to do just mildly amusing. Kerry only cared about Joe's rudeness when it pertained to her mom. She couldn't handle anyone treating her mother like that, or saying anything insulting about her.

> *Obviously your only source of information (besides your own imagination) is my father. I just hope you realize all guys are like him, and will say whatever they want just to get a blow job. I feel sorry for you.*
>
> *By the way, stop saying "our" father because I only have one sister, and it's not your dirty little ass. You can't just pick a guy your whore mother slept with and decide he's the one that will be your dad.*
>
> *And stop whining about money, and just respect MY dad for getting so much out of you guys. You really must be stupid or just that gullible if you can't live your own day to day because of how much you gave him. He has money, doesn't need it from you idiots no matter what you say. He makes about $70,000 a year. He's just an idiot with money, and spends it*

before he has it, gambles, drinks too much, all the shit he shouldn't do. But, that's MY mom's problem, and doesn't concern you two, because you're not family. I work, he works, my mom doesn't only because he doesn't want her to; he LOVES coming home to her, NOT your mother. Must be a reason for that, don't you think? And I moved to Montana without any money from him! I am where I am today because of my own hard work. Maybe you and your mother should try that!

Don't blame the fact that you're broke on us. If your mother wouldn't have been with a married man and found her own, you'd have a father to help with your bills. And like I said, it's her stupidity for giving him the money. Men in this family have ways of women wanting to give them shit, but your mother is the first who actually thought she was getting some of it back.

Are you proud that you gave him money to get out of jail? Good for you, you wasted more money that you'll never see again.

And the comments you made about my mother are ridiculous. I have friends MY age who wanted her, and she's mistaken for my sister on a regular basis because she looks so young. Do you ever get that—didn't think so. And she does it by exercise—ever heard of it?

My mother wasn't the one to call the cops that night, even though she should have told them at the hospital. Her friends did because it wasn't the first time my dad was a drunken asshole and hit my mom. Their problems, not hers.

That's funny you think I'm messed up since you think you'll someday have a brother and sister. And you don't even know me, and you never will, because luckily Montana is a hell of a distance from North Carolina. And when was the last time I was even in your screwed up little town? When I do go home to see my parents, I'm still a good hour away from your dirty little hut in the woods.

You keep saying you have the right to a family, good luck finding one, since you keep trying to steal mine. Your mother can't sleep around and pick and choose which man should support her. My dad has obviously made his decision about what woman he wants to spend his days, and NIGHTS, with, because he's not at your house!

You saying I'm ugly is amusing, considering everyone says I look just like "our" father. And he's often asked when I'll stop being such a popular guy and settle down, because I get so many dates. I'll make sure to visit you and your mother in ten years or so, when you'll be working at the closest grocery store, bagging the canned goods.

Bye bye.

9

It did not take long to allow facts to set in. Kerry was an only child and she lived in, and would always live in, a single-parent home. When her biological father finally resurfaced in North Carolina, he went back to Acacia. Angelica did not handle it well at all, but that did not surprise Kerry, because she knew this was pretty much the answer to their future. Him being gone for a time, everyone blatantly seeing him abusing his wife. She knew if he came back and went back to his wife instead of coming to her, then she would never have a chance at a future with him. Love is cruel, no matter what anyone says. Kerry's guilt ate at her, because she prayed as often as her mother did, but it wasn't for Calvin to come home to them. She prayed he would either never come home or never speak to them again. She almost felt bad when her prayer came true and her mother's didn't, but she knew it was for the best. Kerry knew the first time he ever rose a hand to her mother, he'd wake up the next day with a hand missing and the toilet clogged.

Angelica cancelled her trip to the beach with her best friend, Hannah, and the other girls from work. She said she couldn't spend any money they didn't have anyway. She was so upset and heartbroken that she kept saying she had nothing now, no money, no life, and now, no heart. It would take time, but Kerry decided she must convince her mother that everything she had lay within her and her daughter. Kerry was by no means a comparison to the love one is supposed to feel for a man, but she was love, nonetheless, and she was her family, and she would always be, no picking and choosing for Kerry. They had been through this all together, not in her mother's heart alone. It was partly Kerry's fault Angelica thought she fought her inner battle alone, because Kerry was such a loner and not a talker, so who could blame her? Kerry still doesn't ask her mother for advice, and she doesn't pretend to be interested in her feelings towards Calvin. She is there for judgment regarding Calvin, and never anything else; any other topic can be discussed openly with advice and planning. Kerry never listened to her when she said how much she loved him, though, and when she said she knew that he "could" be a great man but just wasn't acting like it. Kerry always felt nothing but pity for her mother in those times, because she couldn't understand why someone would want to be with such a loser. Time heals all wounds, sometimes LOTS of time, but it does anyway, and it took forever for her mom's wounds to heal, but when they did, they were unbreakable.

After a few days of missing work, Angelica's boss was frustrated and refused to grant any more vacation or sick days. Her mental recovery was a slow recuperation, and after crying with Hannah, the beach trip was back on. She would be gone for the last three days she had off. Kerry just hoped this would help her forget how horrible it was to imagine Calvin on his knees begging Acacia for forgiveness, telling her that the only family that ever meant anything to him was her and their children. Telling her that Kerry was merely a mistake, and that her mother meant nothing to him.

10

Angelica came home refreshed and ready to return to the real world. Until she got there. Her boss was serious and gave her an ultimatum, even though her boss knew of the "family history" Angelica lived with daily. Angelica swallowed her pride and asked for a part-time position, and less cases (she was a social worker), accepting a pay-cut, loss of vacation days, and all that came with it. That was not an option and they gave her an ultimatum. She remains at her current position, current case-load and hours (miserable and in terrible mental anguish) or she quits. She went home crying again, and as Kerry held her, she admitted she had to go job-hunting in the morning. The tunnel they were lost in seemed to get longer and darker by the day.

After fifteen years, Angelica wasn't even sure what the job market was like outside of her old "family." She wasn't familiar with doing a resume, applying for anything, admitting why she had to leave her old job, and how to act during an interview. Kerry wanted to help so badly, but who would hire a fifteen-year-old girl? After two weeks of searching, her mother landed a low-paying and low-hours job as a secretary for a local magistrate. Kerry was happy and proud of her for finding a job in a seemingly short period. The money would be a huge blow since she made twice this pay at her old job, and her savings had been gone since Calvin had first started needing money, but luckily Kerry's grandmother was very close and very helpful. Kerry hated herself, and she hated what her biological father had done to her, but mostly to her mother. If he had stayed away, she would still wonder who he was and imagine this great, glorious, generous, handsome man who would someday sweep her mother and herself off their tired, aching feet and out of debt into a huge house with no mortgage on it. She wanted her grandfather back.

It didn't take long for Angelica to move upward in her secretarial position there to running most of the office; after all, she did have fifteen years of people-related experience, mostly in management, and her office organizational skills turned this magistrate's office into a slick working machine. It also did not take long for Calvin to miss his dangerous interludes with his mistress. Being pathetically, yet deeply in love with him, and desperate to please him, she remained at his beck and call. Kerry was not kind or loving at all to him when he called and she was out of her dear mother's earshot. Without her there to monitor Kerry's words about and to Calvin, she was blunt and honest with him. The more he called, the more Kerry decided that she'd never allow herself to fall under any man's spell, so as not to be stuck in such a shitty situation as her mother was. It was almost fun to be mean to him, because he sounded so confused. Especially if he happened to call twice in a day, once while her mom was home and once while she wasn't. He sounded more confused the more Kerry spoke with him, yet he never asked her about it, never tried to be more of a father, nothing. His thoughts were obvious; he didn't understand, but didn't care either. His only concern was getting Angelica into bed every so often, and he had no desire to even try to assist in raising another child, especially one he really did consider a mistake. Not a single effort was ever made that didn't involve just keeping his mistress happy. And Kerry knew her mom would hate to be involved in any sentence that involved the word mistress, but like Kerry said and believed, love makes even the strongest person vulnerable, and sometimes stupid, and puts you in an inescapable place that you can't get out of.

11

Kerry can still remember one afternoon when her mom was at work, and *he* called drunk off his ass. He asked Kerry what she wanted from him. She wasn't sure what to tell him: be serious because he was, or be obnoxious because he was drunk and wouldn't remember anyway? She decided to assume he was joking, so she told him she wanted the off-road truck that was being displayed at the dealership near her home. He laughed in an almost evil way, and began to ask Kerry if she thought he enjoyed the knowledge that he was her father. For once in her life, Kerry was speechless. He finally yelled at her, "I never asked for you! You were the biggest mistake I have ever made, and I should sue the condom company, but if you're so damn desperate to get me to stop trying to be your father, try not having one!"

Kerry sat there holding the dead line, not knowing what to think, say, or do. Her first thought was that she couldn't believe he even considered himself a father to anyone, especially her, which he just blatantly stated was his biggest mistake! Her temper fired up before any tears could threaten her eyes, and she looked at the phone and heard the consistent beeps that meant he had hung up. She threw the cordless into the closest wall, immediate relief flooding over her at the smashing sound. Trying to hold herself together, she got up, still fighting tears she was sure Calvin was unworthy of, and still unsure of how to cope with his evil words. Should they be a relief because she had wanted him out of her life anyway? Should they be ignored because he was drunk? It was one thing to think he hated her, and another to hear him state the fact in plain English. Another thought made Kerry choke down her tears. "Dads" were men who actually knew their children's interests, favorite restaurant, or their sex, for God's sake. Calvin barely knew Kerry was a girl, so why would he even believe he was anything like a father to her? She picked up the cordless, replaced the battery that had flown off, and called her mother at work. She could barely understand Kerry as she was still holding back tears, and her anger made her stumble through the explanation, but when she finally understood, she was furious. She did her best to calm Kerry, and then she said she was in the middle of setting up a court date for someone and would call right back. A few seconds later, the phone rang. Anticipating her mother, she answered the phone eagerly. To her dismay, it was Calvin again. Kerry cursed them not being able to afford caller ID. She asked why he had hung up on her, as this was one of her biggest pet peeves.

"Because you don't want me to be your father," was the drunken response Kerry received. She admitted to him that she had never said that (to him), but he argued that she did not have to say it for it to be true. Fighting back tears of anger, hurt, and deception, she dejectedly retaliated. "If you want it to be true so damn bad, FINE! I hate you more than anything or anyone, and I NEVER want you to call here again!"

Kerry finally burst into tears and threw the phone again. After her repeated conversations with a drunken Calvin, she was at that point where she truly believed people tell the truth when they are past drunk, because their guard is down and their courage up, and their inhibitions thrown to the wind. Basing this on all those previous conversations and actions Calvin showed, he proved her theory that she couldn't believe that she really was a mistake. She could not understand what she had done that was so wrong. Did her mother feel the same way? Had she ruined any chance her mother had at a bright future by showing up on an ultrasound? She robbed her mother's liquor cabinet (under the sink to the left, behind all the candy dishes) and was drunk and in bed before she got home from work. She ignored all knocks on the door, and the next day she told her mother nothing he said mattered, because he was drunk. Her mother let it drop, and didn't say anything about the alcohol missing. Like father, like daughter, Kerry cringed.

One time, he showed up at their house, in a desperate attempt to get Kerry to speak to him and make peace, because even fake peace with Kerry meant no bitching from Angelica. He gave Kerry a one-hundred dollar bill. He kept saying over and over, "I love you, you know that, right?"

Kerry assumed the bill was counterfeit, and checked it thoroughly before going shopping. When she turned sixteen, he told Angelica he wanted to be the one to get Kerry her first car, because he had done that with his other children. She almost said it wasn't worth it because she wasn't one of them, but she bit her tongue. He got Kerry a little pickup truck with big tires, and she thought he had redeemed himself, but threw that thought out of her head; a vehicle does not make up for almost ten years of being an asshole. Especially when Kerry found out that the truck loan was in her mother's name. Which, since she had recently gotten a job, she immediately took the loan booklet and made the payments herself. Nothing from Calvin ever meant anything to her, and this was no different, and she would not accept that her mother was going to have to pay once again for something Calvin merely pointed to and said, "I want that." After asking about the car, Angelica sadly told Kerry the truth about other "gifts" from him, and where they had been purchased, by whom, and if the money was ever reimbursed. Most of the time it was not, especially if the amount went over a hundred bucks.

Kerry reflected, and decided her entire childhood wasn't rained on by misery, as it so seemed until now. She had, and still has, a wonderful family. From her awesome grandmother, funny and generous uncles, down to her loving aunt. They spoiled Kerry rotten, until she almost thought it was something they did merely trying to make up for Calvin, but she learned as she got older she was just their baby. Not just to

Angelica, but to all of them. She was part of a spark that was almost put out when Pappy passed away, but Kerry was the one who kept some of it burning, and kept their lives interesting. Still, Kerry has that "dad" chip on her shoulder, much as she tried to eliminate it. They would do an awesome job of keeping her happy and making sure she was loved, but there was always something missing. And her mom, giving her everything and making her stronger in heart and mind. She didn't bother with many friends, and she was pretty much a loner at school. She was the fat kid, and most of the students let her know it, you know, in case she didn't own a mirror, but she could always go home. Go home to Paul, Wesley, Janine, Grammy, and Mommy. And it was like a different country. Not the real world. A happier place than the real world. Where her age didn't matter, her weight didn't matter, her clothes being in style didn't matter, she was still popular there, she was still loved there. She was only miserable alone. At home, this was fine, but anywhere else, this was not easy to a loner.

12

Kerry's diary:
I feel so strange. It's not exactly a new feeling, but it's been so long since I have felt this way that it's strange. I feel like the world is closing in. Like I have no one to tell this feeling of insanity to, or to explain why I am feeling this way. I have friends, some best friends I tell almost everything to, but I do not want them to worry about me. So I keep this to myself, and I wonder why exactly I feel this way. I am dizzy wondering how I got myself into this mess, and contemplate how I can get out of it. I wonder how people can think they are in love, but they fight, hurt each other physically and mentally, and then they pretend nothing is wrong. When in fact everything that possibly can go wrong has...or will in the near future. Love is not patient, kind, gentle, or nurturing, it is hurtful and harsh, and it likes to bite you in the ass right when you are at your happiest. I actually think that is how you know you love someone, when you always take his or her shit and you never complain. When all you can think of is, what did I do to make them yell and hit? What can I do to apologize and make them love me again? Love isn't understanding, or there would be no fights. They would just know what is wrong, and they would immediately make it right, not fight about it, and tell you how wrong you are and how stupid you are. You can love your parents and hate them at the same time, and whether you know it or not, you still love them while you hate them. Because once you love someone, you can't hate them. You can hate something they have said, or something they have done, but you can't hate them. After a

breakup, though, and you get over that person, and you decide it wasn't worth the time it takes to spit off of a bridge, you realize you didn't feel love. It was lust, or passion, but not love. Love is the strangest emotion, because it pops up and pretends to be some other emotion, like hatred or jealousy. You can hate someone so much, but it's actually love. In reality, you hate their actions, or their words, not them. I hate my father, but it is actually some form of love (I think it's the kind that you have when you know you're related to someone...not the kind that actually MEANS something). Because "dads" know their kids' birthdays, some even plan the parties, and he is nothing like those dads, he doesn't even deserve the title father. He treats me like lint...you can't do anything about it; you just keep picking it out of your pockets and throwing it away. But it's always there, and it just keeps coming back, no matter how hard you try to rid yourself of the problem. That's how my Calvin is with me. He calls me when he has to, you know, to remind me he remembers my phone number, and my name, and in order to make sure he keeps peace with me so he can keep in touch with Mom. He talks to me like I am one of his many customers, trying to sell me off. He is one of those accountants that is sneaky and gets their big accounts to invest in stupid shit, then he earns money off of their failures, so he is practiced at lying and manipulation. "Sure, this item is going to top the sales charts" translates into "Sure we'll have lunch sometime." I have not seen him since Christmas, and it's now June. My 18th birthday has passed...I got a card with a $20 bill in it. Payoff for one of the most important birthdays in my life. Contact is crucial, letters, cards, pictures...all have to be sent to his job, or his wife might see them, and she would not be happy about it. We can't do anything to make his queen unhappy, or the kingdom will fall apart. I feel like a cartoon character with evil stepsisters torturing her, except I never clean, and I'm not wearing a size one rag dress. That, and the fact that my half-sister and half-brother say I do not exist. My friends, well, the ones who know my father isn't dead, want me to talk to Calvin and explain how I feel about all this. The friends I'm not that close to, or just never had the energy to discuss my past with, really think my "charming, loving father" died in a car accident. I have tried to talk to him though, and he must speak a different language, because it doesn't get through his thick man skull. I say I want to spend time with him so we can get to know each other...he takes me to a money-managing conference. He also drove his brother's motorcycle, and I am not sure how many of you have been on a bike with another person, but not much conversation can be had. It is mostly praying you trust them enough not to wreck. I was horrified. I loved motorcycles, but I did not trust Calvin at all. Why should I? What reasons has he given me to trust him with five dollars, much less with my life? I fell for that only once...we went to that conference, and he talked to me probably a total of one minute throughout the course of the day. However long it took to ask me if I was hungry (yes I am), and what would I like to eat? I did not answer him; I told the waitress that one. At least then I would be sure to get what I wanted.

13

Mark had grown very far from Kerry in their latter high school years. His friends were older and much more popular when he joined the football team, and Kerry was included in their "dirty" group. She didn't care, but Mark wouldn't talk to her in front of them, or he would pass her notes behind their backs. His girlfriend had a tally of how many days Kerry had been "dirty" on her notebook. They called her names and pointed and laughed, or just called her out sometimes. She ignored this, she didn't really care anyway, and it really just bothered her that Mark was not sticking up for her. What had happened to their million years of friendship and best friend bullshit? She wrote him a note, because when she called his house, he was on the other line with someone popular, could she call him back? What pissed her off, though, was when something traumatic happened, he *did* come to her. Why was she only good enough when his life was shit? Her letter to him stated the exact same thing; she wanted the simple rights to be his friend no matter who was around and no matter what they thought of her, or nothing at all. She didn't want anyone to be her friend only when it was convenient. His little friends graduated and never spoke to him again once they were in college, so that washed over, and though it still bothered her, she let it pass by with brave colors. It had not been the first shun from Mark she had encountered; it was tough having a best friend who was a boy. Mary had been his girlfriend the year before, and Kerry was pushed away then too, but she didn't mind it then, because he had spoken to her like a human being when Mary was around. But with the latest crew, Mary had been dumped, so she started talking to Kerry.

LIVING AS A MISTAKE

Mary became Kerry's best friend, and they came closer together because Kerry wanted to party and have fun all the time, and because Mark dumped Mary. She wanted to get out and have fun just as much as Kerry did. They came closer together because of a freak car accident, and stayed close after that.

It had felt like it had to be a dream. Mary and Kerry went to get Mary something to eat, and then headed to Kerry's house. Kerry could remember telling her that they had plenty of time to get her home because her father did not get off work until 9:15 and it was only 8:23 on the little clock Kerry had bought. Kerry hit the pothole turning left at the light, again, and made the first left-hand turn onto Cemetery Road. It was such a habitual motion, she didn't even think about it anymore. She had been driving for a year and ten months, and lived on Cemetery, so she had driven the road many thousand times. She felt she had the motions down pat. She knew every curve, how fast she could go on those curves, and every pothole, nook, and cranny in the road. She prided herself on that. She was confident that if anything should ever happen to her on this road, it would be a force of nature, like a deer on the road or something. Anyway, instead of driving like fifty or sixty and driving in the middle, she drove like fifty or sixty and hugged the curb a bit too much. Well, they slid in the gravel instead of driving through it. She knew she was skidding, so she turned the steering wheel toward the road. She jerked it too much, she realized later, but she panicked. She had to have done something else wrong, but she never could pinpoint it. It felt like a dream, like a game or a movie that wasn't real. It was so exciting because it felt so much like a dream; it was the most horrible head rush Kerry had ever felt. She was excited and scared, and was panicked. She was right, though; she jerked the wheel too far, much too far and much too fast. She pressed the gas pedal because she remembered being told that you never slam your brakes in a skid, and they were on the other side of the road before Kerry knew what was happening. She had probably heard that skid thing on a cartoon or something, but she did it anyway, because it was

43

all she had at that moment. She really felt she would pull out of the skid, and she worked the wheel to accomplish this. She almost made it, but when she realized that she was on the wrong side of the road, she swerved the wheel again, back towards the road. It did not work out for the best. They went across the road, and then everything went black for Kerry. The air bag popped out, and Kerry blacked out. She realized later she never heard anything in its true volume. She thought she heard Mary screaming, but it was far, far away. Like in a movie coming from another room of a house. She never heard the back window shatter, and she never heard the little window behind the driver's seat shatter. She never felt the glass fall all over her. It even went into her coat pockets, but she never noticed it. Was she passed out? She did not hear the crunch of the hood or of the trunk, and she never felt the pain course through her upper body. It was so surreal. The next thing she heard and felt was Mary. Mary prodded her and said that they had to get out of the car fast and now. Kerry shook her head, as if drugged, and looked around. She saw the air bag, now deflated a little, and then saw the smoke. It looked like it was coming out of the ignition. The doors automatically locked when the car was in gear, so they felt they couldn't get the doors open fast enough. Kerry never noticed that hers was ajar the whole time. It had been forced open in the crash. Her seatbelt was stuck, and in a panic, she pulled it out away from her body to slide out of it without actually unhooking it. Mary still had a hold of her as she climbed out the window on her side and around the tree branches hanging in her way. Kerry crawled towards her, inadvertently putting her hands on her CD case. Not even thinking about it, she grabbed onto them and took them out the window with her. The car was still running, and all the lights were on, hazard, oil, check engine, all of them. The CD player that Angelica had paid big bucks for never even skipped. And it was still playing.

 The icy water rushed into both of their sneakers quickly as their feet met the ground. They landed in a creek, barely enough water in it to call it a stream. Yet there was enough water in it to soak both of them up to their knees. The headlights shone up into the trees unnaturally. Kerry did not even notice the missing windows or the dents that were all over her baby. The girls crawled up onto the road. Kerry noticed how far they had gone off the road into the water. It had to have been over ten feet. It doesn't seem like much, but it was. She pulled her cell phone out of her pocket, getting small scratches from the glass, and brushed the pieces of glass off of the phone, and, unsurprisingly, it had no service, so she shoved it back into the glass-filled pocket. They decided to head up the hill where they had come from. It was not until Kerry turned around and saw the odd way that the car was sitting in the ditch that she started to cry. She cried about her car, about the money it would cost to have it fixed, and how her Mom was going to kill her. They both evaluated themselves, never asking aloud if the other was okay. Kerry believed if she assumed she was okay, then so was Mary. And since Mary never asked, Kerry believed she thought the same thing. Their only complaints turned out to be that Mary had an ugly bump on her leg and Kerry's chest ached horribly. It hurt to breathe and even more to cry. But she did both, as the pain was much worse inside her head rather than outside. Mary tried to reassure her, but it was Kerry's *car, her only* source of *freedom*, and the pain lasted longer than that night. Nothing she could have said would have made Kerry feel better. Because she knew, no matter how much gravel was on the road, and how slippery it was from the sprinkles of rain, it still would have happened. It was her fault and she knew it. However, she did not want anyone else to know that. She did not want them to know how much she blamed herself. There really was too much gravel on the road (now, but that could also be because of the accident) and she could not help that, but she always drove too fast. She could have helped that. They did not get far walking. Kerry kept turning around to see if her car had changed in any way. She's still not sure what she expected, but nothing happened. She could still hear the music. The show had played on. The tears coursed down her cheeks. She wasn't sure what to think and she knew all her thoughts were muddled together. It all hurt so badly. She loved her car, seriously. It was her whole life; her escape from sadness was to get in her car and just go, nowhere special, just drive around listening to music with the windows down and the cool air streaming in. She had just killed her only escape. And to think that it was in a wreck on a curve she was told many times to slow down on just made things worse. Her Uncle Paul had wrecked in almost the same place quite a long time ago.

Reflecting, she got her permit on the day she turned sixteen, and got her first pickup later that day. It was one of the greatest days in her shitty little miserable life. Until some dumb-ass wrecked into her pickup, which actually ended up good, because she met Belle, but that's another story. Anyway, after that first wreck totaled her old pickup, she got her baby, her poor baby. She had picked it out with her mom and with her Uncle Wesley, and since her Uncle Wesley's opinion was like gold to her, he had helped her treat that car like glass and took extra special care of it, mechanically and body-wise, until today. Kerry hated herself every time she looked back and saw the illuminated trees from the headlights. Then, she saw the headlights coming from down the road. They were coming from the opposite way that they had started walking, so those people would see the car before they would see two girls walking. In a panic, Kerry turned and ran, wincing against the pain, running from Mary, and she started screaming. More parts started hurting from running, but she just kept going, and kept screaming. She screamed at the mini-van to get away from her car. She still has no idea why she was yelling, and she did not think she could stop herself, but her throat ached as the screams kept coming out again and again. The headlights stopped, and Kerry saw a couple in the van with their children. She ran past the woman who was out asking if they were okay. She ran to her car, crying harder as she got closer.

Mary came over to Kerry and put her arm around her seemingly mentally paralyzed best friend, trying to soothe her. She was still crying as the sweet, worried man asked what the girl's home number was so he could call their parents. Kerry told him her home number, after all they were in her car, and Mary's father was still at work, yet the whole time Kerry still moaned about her baby. Mary told him to let Kerry talk to her mother, so Angelica wouldn't panic at the sound of a man's voice telling her about her daughter in a wreck. When Angelica answered, Kerry lost all use of words; she did not tell her what happened. She just told her to come to where Uncle Paul had wrecked before. She told her she did not want to tell her over the phone, just to come. The woman in the van put her arm around Kerry as she stood and cried before the pieces of car. Angelica and Uncle Paul were there in a second, since it's a stone's throw from home. Kerry ran to her, crying about the car. Angelica was horrified all Kerry cared about was the car, and she told her beloved daughter not to worry about the car, and asked how the Kerry was. She reassured Kerry that nothing else mattered as long as she and Mary were okay. Her Uncle Paul, usually not an emotional person, looked very concerned and hugged Kerry tightly. Kerry thought about everything, and although nothing changed about how depressed she was about her car, she thought about how she was standing there and not getting in an ambulance, and she held onto her mother and uncle very tightly.

After everybody left and her Uncle Wesley came to tow the car home, Kerry went into her grammy's house and hugged both her grandmother and her aunt. She thanked God she could hug them, and that she wasn't unconscious and being hauled off to the nearest hospital. Her family hauled her and Mary off to the hospital afterwards, just as a precaution, with X-rays and all that fun stuff. On the way home from the hospital, Kerry cried some more, but for more realistic reasons. She drove to school because of work after school; her mom had a job, and her uncles had jobs too. She hated herself for making another bill for her mom to have to worry about. She just thanked God that Mary and she had made it out okay; it was the anniversary of Pappy's death, and that made a difference in her mind.

Any other day, it would have been a bad wreck, but she believed in fate, and in angels, and her Pappy watched over her best friend and her that night.

14

 Time for graduation already? Hard to believe eighteen came so quickly. In this time, Kerry had the great blessing of meeting Belle, when the boy Belle was dating wrecked into Kerry's pickup. They stayed close after meeting, and Belle became one of the few people that Kerry actually let into her life, telling her all about her past, present, and dreams of the future. By this time, there were only three friends that Kerry had given that opportunity to, and of course Mark was one, because he was there for all of it. Belle became the third, after Kerry met Candie on the bus in seventh grade. Candie was one of Kerry's rare moments of bravery and courage, as she spoke to her on her first day in the school that was all new to Candie. Kerry loved that she found someone new, someone that the popular people hadn't already intimidated into hating her and making fun of her, and it was great to have someone to spend so much time with. They rode the bus together, had the same homeroom, and Candie was excited to let Kerry show her all around Raeford, North Carolina. It wasn't much of a town, very small and insignificant in comparison to the big cities around it, but it had been Kerry's home all of her life, and she was eager to finally let someone into her world. Kerry had waited so long to finally fit in with a crowd, even if it was a very small crowd. Kerry wasn't handling being a senior very well, though, and her drinking was still pretty regular, the stealing of her mother's liquor becoming quite often, and mostly to the point where she had to find someone to buy her bottles to hide in her room. This way her mother would question her less about where the booze was going at such an alarmingly fast rate. This is also when she started smoking. She started when she wasn't able to get a drink one time, but had the opportunity to buy cigarettes instead. Kerry was eager to graduate, and her applications to college were in and everything was set up for her to start college in the fall, just a junior college, but she was hoping to meet people who didn't judge her as much as her high school classmates did.

What I Learned from High School...

I learned how to copy homework and not get caught.
I learned how to tell a convincing lie.
I learned how to be strong enough not to cry, and not to show emotion.
I learned how not to care, at least not when people are around.
I learned how to be a wallflower.
I learned how to become that wallflower whenever convenient.
I learned how to become sarcastic enough to get myself into trouble.
I learned how to let people think they are being trusted.
I learned how to be a bitch.
I learned how to misjudge people because of previous bad experiences.
I learned how to decipher between good and bad, and still make the wrong decision.
I learned how to get out of the consequences of that wrong decision.
I learned how to take a shot of vodka, like a man, and not even flinch.
I learned how it feels to crave alcohol.
I learned how to pretend not to be drunk.
I learned how to inhale a cigarette.
I learned how to drive way too fast.
I learned how to handle my car when I shouldn't even be driving in the first place.

*I learned how to say no, eventually.
I learned lessons that will stay with me for life.
I learned how to tell my mom the truth.
I learned how to really trust someone with your life.
I'm glad I learned the bad along with the good, even if I couldn't tell them apart at the beginning.*

    Belle almost changed some very hidden things about Kerry. She was so polite, kind, and loving, she nearly suffocated you with her affections. Before leaving her, she would give hugs and kisses, and always tell you she loved you. It was all new to Kerry to meet someone who showed their love so openly, and she allowed Kerry to open up to her in a trusting manner. She was younger than Kerry was, so anytime she wanted to spend time with Belle, she had to pick her up, which was another tragic thing about the car being crashed, because Kerry was isolated from the only person who opened up Kerry's heart. But, stubborn, trusting Belle, she would hitchhike to Kerry's house, anything to find a way there. She was Kerry's rock, never failing to make her smile, or to have a drink with her, and she always was there. There aren't very many friends that people can lean on no matter what, but Belle always did that. She nearly drove Kerry nuts with her attention, but she was the type of person everyone fell in love with. They couldn't go anywhere within three counties without her seeing at least three people she knew. And she always ran up to them and hugged them, and chatted for a few minutes, always introducing Kerry, even though Kerry was usually a little nervous, because she never had those types of friends. Kerry was used to surrounding herself with people like her, who enjoyed being isolated, and hung out with the wallflowers, making fun of people who actually were popular, but Belle was one of the rare people that gave everyone her love. What Kerry liked most about Belle was the fact that she refused to judge anyone. She was not a fan of Calvin, but she never spoke unkindly of him. She just politely listened to Kerry complain and call him names, then she'd mix a drink or tell a joke. Always smiling and happy, Kerry was grateful to have her around. She was the only person who could make her believe in herself, and Kerry always considered her an angel.

15

After a few years of little contact, and her eighteenth birthday passing with no contact, Kerry wrote Calvin a letter, sending it to his workplace.

This letter is not going to be easy to write. Words aren't a big thing for you, though, and you have a way of weaseling out of whatever you do wrong. I am tired of pretending you are a good father figure and I am done pretending you care. I have tried to be patient and forgiving, but I have had it. I am through with this load of shit you have been feeding me since I was seven. Let us recap, shall we, Father, dear? I met you when I was seven, a day I will never forget. I was blessed with a full family then; you were the piece I had never found. However, with you came three extra pieces I had never counted on. I was okay with that though, it did not bother me one bit. The more the merrier, right? WRONG! I have a half-sister and a half-brother who will never ever accept me as human much less a relative of theirs, and a woman who despises me more than Satan. She knows nothing about me, and never will, and you have never tried to change that. The many promises you broke (or conveniently forgot) I forgive you for. I forgive you for the lies, the hurt, and the anger. What doesn't kill you makes you stronger, right? Well, you have come closer than you think to killing me many times. But, I have survived, and I intend to. I remember you promising me phone calls, meals, help paying my bills, love. Want to remember what I've received? I have a pretty decent memory here: one Christmas, I got a Barbie car, sweatshirt, a musical figurine; one birthday a truck...no, wait. You actually have to pay for all of those to count. I am happy you picked the truck out, but wasn't very upset when someone hit it, and I had the opportunity to get a vehicle with my uncle, a man who actually loves me and cares for me. I have expected way too much out of you, and for that, I'm sorry. I have a million pictures of me and my mom, though, and about three of you and me. We've eaten maybe ten meals together, rode in a car together maybe twenty-five times, and spoken maybe 150 times. In twelve years. Pathetic if you ask any other father. What have I ever asked you for? Love. Attention. Now, I ask for nothing. Ever again. For my 18th birthday, a birthday my mother called the most important (my golden birthday because I was 18 on the 18th), you didn't even bother to call me, much less visit me. And then for my graduation, once again you didn't show, and didn't even bother to call. Everyone there with their proud parents and loved ones, and I had my mom, grammy, and my best friend, Candie. Mark's sister flew up from Florida for him, and you couldn't drive an hour for your youngest child. Oh! Sorry, I'm just a mistake, and was never a child. And now I am 18. My uncle, who lives in Raleigh, remembered and sent me a card. Not much, but it said, "Love, Unk Ben." My mom, gram, uncles, aunts, cousins, and friends celebrated with me. Even your mom remembered and sent me a card. I know you claim you like to hand people their cards or gifts, but it is truly a disgrace to totally disregard my birthday. I still have not heard from you. Not even a phone call.

So, here is my early present for you: I'm letting you go. I am giving you up. You no longer have to pretend you miss me and care about me. I realize I must have been a hassle to you for my 18-year existence, but I am a blessing to my mother. There, give Acacia a hug and a kiss. I am sure she will be thrilled. It is what the two of you have always wanted. I am relieving myself of any further heartache. I have taken my fill of pain from you. I cannot handle any more. If you leave now, you cannot hurt me anymore.

    He didn't call, so Kerry was never truly sure he received the letter, because she doubted he would have contacted her after his child support payments were done anyway, but she never heard another word from him. He called Angelica every once in awhile, when the mood woke him, but why call Kerry? She was just his mistake. It suited her fine, the less she spoke with him, the less had to pretend she loved him. Angelica quit trying to get her to speak with him, as she read that letter prior to Kerry mailing it, and she let Kerry know that since she had Wesley and Paul, she would let her go, because they were more to Kerry than Calvin could have ever been anyway.

16

After all the insurance crap was over and done with from Kerry's little escapade into the watery depths, she found a used car to call her own. It wasn't the same, but at least she had her chance to escape again. She was, after all, the driver in the excursions that her and Mary went on. More recently, they had started partying in a neighboring town, after they met Cameron. Cameron and Kerry really did not know each other long before she felt some kind of connection. She didn't let him know that though, guys get weird when they think emotions are involved. She met him at Mark's graduation party. He was such a punk with his spikey bracelets, and yet so adorable with his black hair that had long streaks of blond in it. He arrived in this ugly brown van, but Kerry thought it might fit materials for a band quite nicely, and for some reason, it seemed to fit him. They talked at the graduation party, but she had promised Mary they would go to this camp party. So, around ten, Cameron actually drove her mom home and they went to pick Mary up. Mark and his girlfriend went with them for this excursion. Mark decided to get everyone to play this game called "take it off" (meaning your clothes), and it was like a little porn wagon after Angelica was safely dropped off at home. At Mary's there were more clothes on the floor of the van than on any one person. Except Kerry, of course, tubby little Kerry refused to take off anything besides her shirt, which she held up against her stomach. She was too embarrassed, especially since it was weird enough with Mark there half naked. Mark even mooned Mary's dad! The man was not happy about that. They dropped Mark and his girlfriend back off at the graduation party, and Kerry asked Cameron if he would like to go to the party with Mary and her. He said he would, and by eleven, they were on their way to the party. They made it at about 2:00 a.m. It was not a typical three-hour drive, but it took them that long for good reason. They thought aliens abducted them. Seriously. Kerry even debated whether she should still speak to Cameron after the abduction, but she continued to "date" him for three months after that. They had turned off the Interstate to a small town called Sellers because it had the little gas station icon on the sign, and they drove around this two-road town for God knows how long (on empty) until they decided the sign was wrong, there was no gas station. So they stopped, at midnight, at the only house with lights on, and asked for some gas. They didn't have any, and the nearest gas station was twenty miles away according to the people. Which they still could not find, and the next one had been forty miles away, not twenty, and it was closed! Unreal! Kerry's gas tank ran for those three hours past the little E that stands for "put gas in, you fool." She had never gone that far without gas, so how else do you explain the fact that they accidentally drove into the next state? They actually had the South Carolina state police escort them to a gas station, because they were still running out as they left North Carolina, and then on their way back home, they passed right through the party. Explain that, they went the exact same way, but not one of three people saw the damn town (with its six gas stations or more) until they had re-entered their home state. Along the lonely stretches of highway, they counted more deer standing on the side, and more raccoons and skunks than any had remembered seeing all year. It was like some kind of weird cartoon where the animals were waiting for one of the girls to sing and pet the birds. Kerry sped past them, because they were creeping her out way too much. Aliens, they seriously believed it.

17

    Cameron got around, so to speak, and took the girls to numerous parties, where they quickly learned not to get close, so as not to get into trouble. You see, you can easily blend into the crowd, have an awesome time, and keep to yourself at the same time. This saves quite a bit of trouble if the cops happen to arrive, and you decide to run for it (sometimes smart, sometimes very stupid). If someone else is caught, what is the first thing the cops ask? Who were you with? They always ask for names, but if you never disclose your last name, or your hometown, you get to slide away while your new "buddy" gets into his own trouble. This was probably wrong of them, but they didn't know these people so who is to say they wouldn't have immediately turned the girls in? Plus, they were more afraid of their parents than new people they could just ditch in the future. They were really just after that one party in the heat of the moment anyway, so the next day they could think of something else to do or someone else to do it with.

    They went to a graduation party out at one of Cameron's buddies' camps. He had told Kerry he would see her after this party, because he figured they needed a night apart from each other, so she was really shocked when he called and asked if they could come out to the campsite. They jumped at the chance to party, because it's always good to have new faces, that way if you get bored with one crew, you go see a different one. They sped to Kerry's house, grabbed clothes and a contact case for when they didn't make it home, and some more money for gas and cigarettes. When they finally arrived at the camp, most of the people were already drunk, and even though they seemed really cool, they made sure to be discreet about themselves. Samuel was one of the guys they met there, who liked Mary, and she made sure to like him too. They had been sitting on this picnic table, and Samuel had sauntered over to them, trashed already, but started asking for the girl's IDs and asking how much they had already drank because he was supposedly going to "haul us in." Kerry and Mary both laughed at him, because he was trying to tell them he was a nineteen-year-old cop. The girls seriously thought he was full of shit until he showed them his badge. After that, they made sure to be a little nicer to him. He was drunk when they got there, so at this party they weren't worried about him arresting them, but he worked in a neighboring town, so they were polite in case he pulled them over for anything else in the future. They ended up getting really wasted that night. They weren't the only ones, some girl jumped in a nearby river, and all they did was laugh because apparently nobody liked her. She had been stealing everyone's drinks so she was not anyone's favorite person that night. And from the people that had known her before that night, it did not seem like they had even invited her. That was just the start of their parties with strangers.

18

One of the most memorable parties and by far one of the best ones was the green pool party. It was at Nathan's house, Cameron's best friend. This was also one of the first parties, but still remains the best. Behind Nathan's house, he had a pool, but since it was still early summer, it was still green. Not just a little green either, it was like...growth and strange algae things inside it green. While Cameron and his two friends went for the beer, Kerry and Mary dared Joe to jump in his pool. He takes off his shirt, and damned if he didn't jump right in! Kerry almost shit, she was so shocked. Mary stood there with her jaw on the lawn, and then burst out laughing. Kerry changed her clothes (green was sure to stain), and jumped in with her leather dog collar on. Wait, let's explain the dog collar. No, Kerry was not into domination or anything, she was just so insecure and unsure of who she really was, that she was chained down, and it had spikes and studs on it, so it gave her a punk look. And since Cameron had that punk thing down, she was really getting into it, and had decided to dye her hair a much blonder sheen with some deep red streaks in it. Since she really had no other look (or at least one within her minimal budget) that fit her at the time, she made her own. Mary had the same thing going on by the way; they were inseparable at the time, remember, and Mary was single. But she, uncaring even then, jumped right into the nasty ass pool. Fully clothed and very oblivious to the disgusting green shit floating in Nathan's water. They swam around for a while, until Mary thought she saw a worm (her ultimate fear would have to be those slimy little buggers) and she was out in two seconds flat. Kerry followed, and ran to her car to get towels. Do not ask why she had towels in her trunk, but when Mary and Kerry were together they discovered you never know what you are going to need. There was also a wardrobe, a blanket, probably some beer, and if you were lucky, a pack of cigarette's. If you were lucky. If they knew there were cigarettes in the trunk, they were gone in minutes. They dried off, still impatiently waiting for the beer, as Kerry observed her best friend flirting with their host. Mary wasn't attached to anyone, other than this little nineteen-year-old cop incident that had happened earlier in the month, so it was okay for her to flirt. It was just funny because he was Kerry's boyfriend. Sometimes anyway. It depended on the mood he was in; sometimes he referred to himself as her boyfriend, and some days he freaked out because Kerry referred to him as her boyfriend. As time wore on with him, Kerry knew she was merely just getting herself into trouble, and she honestly suspected he was a little into guys. Something like that anyway; she was pretty sure he was more mentally screwed up than she was. Anyway, he was Cameron's best friend, which was an odd couple if you ever saw one. Cameron with his punk spikes, and his baggy jeans and chains hanging, and piercing on any place that would hold a piece of jewelry, and then Nathan, who looked like the most popular boy at school, the one who got the good grades, was still hot, and was the best choice to take home to Mom and Dad. They just didn't see to fit into each other's lives, but they did.

    Since Nathan and the girls had green pool shit all throughout their hair and pores, they all climbed in the shower (fully clothed) with Nathan. He was nearly in ecstasy with the idea of being in the shower with two eighteen-year-old girls, but they just laughed. They were still dressed after all. The beer still not at the party yet, they tossed their soggy clothes in the dryer and waited. Impatiently, might be added. They checked out Nathan's dad's motorcycle (one of Kerry's passions was bikes), and Nathan even gave her a ride, where she just acted exactly how she felt. Free. The wind blowing in her hair, a strong man in front of her, and she felt so crazy she even flashed the neighbors, which he found hilarious. He even let her drive, showing her where the gears and clutch were, his hands over hers as he showed her how to accelerate the bike. Kerry let her hair fly behind her into Nathan's face, and she drove fast and hard around curves, easily adjusting to the idea of driving a motorcycle, impressive since she learned with a passenger. When she returned from her riding lesson, eager to get a raise so she could purchase one of her own very soon, finally the beer had arrived. The two of them practically ran to the car, chasing Mary down the driveway and hurried to get the beer inside the house. Mary ended up getting even more toasted than Kerry was. Not that she would remember. Chris and John, Cameron's beer buddies, taught Kerry and Mary how to play Circle of Death as soon as the beer arrived.

Aces up to tens that are black you drink, aces up to tens that are reds, you give out to the other players to drink. Jacks are rhymes (pick a word and pray nobody can rhyme with it, whoever doesn't has to drink), Queens are types (pick, for example, brands of cigarettes and whoever can't name one has to drink), and Kings, now Kings are fun. Whoever is the King, gets to make a rule. A really hilarious rule to make is that everyone that has to drink has to say "I am so constipated" right before they drink. Amazingly, after a few cans of beer, this sentence is the most hilarious thing you've ever heard. Especially since it goes around the table with everyone stating blatantly how sincerely and abnormally constipated they were. Kerry took Cameron's stupid baggy belt with the spikes on it and wore it after a few beers, because by then she felt she was cool. Then later in the evening, she was wearing his sweatshirt with all the holes in it, and his fishnet-type wrist guards in addition to his belt, because by then, she felt she was invincible to the world. The fun was just starting as the game continued, and another game started, and a case of beer was gone. Blurs from this night still haunt Kerry's sober mind, and some still make her laugh. After one case of beer was gone, the crew decided to move the party outside. In the garage, they started a great game of beer pong, which is played on a pong table (preferably, but if none is available any old table will do) with six cups filled with beer to a team. These cups are placed in a triangle at the end of the table. Also, a cup with water should be there to clean the ping-pong ball. The player takes a pong ball (required) and bounces it into the cups. If they make it into one, a player on the other team has to chug that beer. Then they get to take a cup of full beer away, and the first team with no cups wins. And this doesn't mean no cups because they had to drink it all. The first team to make the other drink all their beer wins. And the losing team is probably buzzed by that time, from all the chugging.

Halfway through the game was when Mary's cell phone rang. It was Samuel, the nineteen-year-old cop. The thing with Samuel was somewhat complicated actually. You see, a party Cameron, Mary, and Kerry went to with Samuel was at his buddy Jack's house. At that party, Mary's mom's car got all jacked up. There weren't that many people at the party, just Jack, his girlfriend Kelly, Jim, some other guy who left really early, Samuel, Mary, Cameron, and of course, Kerry. They did a pretty bad job on Mary's mom's sedan too; they ripped a symbol off, bent the antenna, bent the license plate in two corners, which amazed the girls, because of the fact that this would be incredibly difficult with bare hands considering the density of the metal (but the drunken assholes probably used pliers), keyed it (probably with the E from SE, because it was missing as well), and they ripped off the windshield wiper. Not just the blade, the entire arm of the wiper. Her father (her mother had passed away when she was three) was furious with her for this happening, and she wouldn't go home for almost four days because of it. Kerry was partially blamed too, because she was the bad influence in Mary's life, and her father hated their friendship. Mary finally went home only because her father threatened to have them arrested for grand theft auto. Looking back, her father had only good intentions, because grand theft auto on their records would definitely have made them change their ways, but at the time, they were just furious with him for judging their partying life. Samuel said he'd find out who did it, but they were supposed to be his friends at that party, so how could he blame them? Anyway, he called Mary because they liked each other, but the whole car thing drove them apart. He wanted her to say that the whole thing happened somewhere else, and she wanted his friends hung from poles. After only a few minutes on the phone with Samuel, she started crying. Cameron tried talking to her while Kerry took the phone and chatted with Samuel herself, mostly drunken knowledge coming out. Nobody was getting any answers, and Nathan was getting impatient because he wasn't getting any. Being the emotional nutcase she was, Kerry was usually the one to cry when she was drunk, so she stayed in an annoying giddy mood that she wasn't even upset or letting anything get to her. She was practically on cloud nine. She had long ago gotten used to being the over-dramatic "crying drunk," but it was intensely nice to her to be the one that acted almost high. She just wanted to relax and barely wanted to bother with anything other than lifting the beer to the mouth. Kerry had a very difficult time to get Samuel to hang up the phone and make sure he wouldn't call back in five minutes, because he wanted to come get the drunk girls, but Kerry refused to let him find out where they were. And she had been careful about telling him who they were with, because she wasn't sure if he knew where Nathan lived. One thing that could be a really bad thing about Samuel was he was a local cop, even if he was only nineteen. There was no way of knowing if he had been drinking, so Kerry wanted him to stay away all night. She decided they were too drunk to be getting caught. Besides, Mary was already crying, what more did they need? After the party started to die down, and the beer was gone, the sickness followed. The one that always hangs out after the beer is gone, and everyone is staggering around giddy. Cameron was throwing up in the garage bathroom first, and then moved into the house because he thought he was done. He wasn't. Kerry gave a meager and pathetic attempt at helping him, but she realized quickly there was nothing she could do, aside from allowing the smell of him to command her stomach to throw up as well. The funniest thing happened while he was dry heaving though. With his head half in the bathroom sink, he muttered, "Dcuo halph a cundom?"

Translated into English, he was trying to ask if Kerry had a condom with her. Kerry just stood there laughing while he vomited. In her drunken stupor she couldn't stop laughing; she actually had to leave the room to get away from him. They had never had sex, but they had talked about it, and it definitely was not the time for it! Kerry would have puked all over him just from his smell. She couldn't believe he was finally ready and he was too drunk to do it anyway. Kerry wasn't the type to "chase tail," but she was frustrated by Cameron's lack of interest in her sexually. She was losing weight finally, probably from never being home to eat, and keggers rarely have a barbeque going, and she still thought she was hideous because he never wanted to have sex. Usually guys in this age group jump at the chance, so Kerry was in a repeated motion of believing she was always going to be fat and ugly. At least this time for Kerry, he remembered saying this after she reminded him the next morning, which just made it even funnier, and allowed her to rub it in his face every day thereafter.

Kerry looked around the living room, saw nobody, then realized with babysitting Cameron, she hadn't seen Mary for a while. She searched everywhere, the garage, all the rooms in the house (and found a few people sleeping who got pissed off when the lights woke them), but did not find Mary. There was only one door locked that she could not get to: Nathan's bedroom. She didn't hear anything, but left before she would have to, thinking that at least someone was getting attention and being made to feel beautiful tonight. Cameron came out of the bathroom looking a bit ragged, and Kerry found a blanket and cuddled up on the couch with him, Kerry facing the front because he did not smell that great.

She woke up the next morning on the floor in the living room. She was wearing Cameron's socks for some odd reason (she really didn't remember putting them on, although she was still wearing the belt and the holey-hoodie), and he was above her on the couch. She could only assume he bumped her off, the stupid fat ass. She had the blanket though, so maybe she moved in the middle of the night. From the smell wafting in her direction from his stinky self, she thought the latter was possible, but since she believes she blacked out for awhile (considering the lack of memories in times of the night before) God only knows. The sounds of the morning clean-up crew rang out in the kitchen and the hallway. Some guy was lying in the bathroom with bread all around him (nobody seemed to know why), and another was in the garage sleeping beside the motorcycle. Kerry kicked Cameron, because he reeked of vomit, beer, and sweat, and she could barely get close enough to kick him without gagging. She couldn't imagine getting close enough to actually touch him. It was bad enough her head was screaming in mind-numbing hangover pain, but she wasn't about to add a stomachache from throwing up stomach acid from lack of food. And stupid Cameron had work today, and Kerry nearly gagged at the thought of all the people who would have the pleasure of eating something he cooked, because he worked at a restaurant at the mall. Kerry finally got herself together enough to help the clean-up crew (it took three industrial-size garbage bags to get the place spotless), and everyone helped Nathan load his luggage into the car. It was amazing how many more people were there. Kerry thought vaguely in the back of her mind that she didn't remember anyone else coming over to drink, which frightened her a bit, but she pushed the thought out of her mind. It would do her mentally-ill mind no good to try to remember when new people, new strangers, had shown up at the house. She was starting to worry about her drinking, but refused to admit she had a problem, and merely attempted to perfect her attempt at driving drunk. There would be no more parties at Nathan's any day soon, as he was off to the airport today, in order to meet his parents at some relative's house. The hangover capital of the world got ready to start its day. Everyone packed up their shit (including the shit from the dryer), and Mary and Kerry dropped Cameron off at work, smelling like shit with some cologne sprayed on it. They actually had to drive him there with all the windows down, as his stench was nose murder. Kerry then dropped Mary off at home, and took her own smelly self home to the shower to prepare for another night of partying.

19

It was around this time that the girls began the process of going to small local towns, attempting to find some new parties, until they started cruising the tiny town of Timberland, full of new and exciting strangers. By cruising, Kerry meant they drove up and down the same few streets of the small town, looking for new faces and new parties. They also started hanging out with Charlie, who became one of the girl's temporary best friends. They really did mean temporary because pretty much whoever was hosting the best, cheapest party was their "best" friend. They used that term lightly as to make the host happy, and it kept them out of trouble and out of debt. Anyway, back to Charlie, he was on the highway one day, heading past Raeford and towards Montrose, and he tried to pass Kerry, but as soon as he was close, she slammed on the gas, flying past him. Looking in the mirror to see if he gave her the finger or not, she noticed it was a guy and a girl, and he was laughing. He turned at the same exit Kerry chose and they continued to race until he pulled over at a gas station to talk to his friends. Kerry slowed down, turned around, and drove up to his four-wheeling machine. They started to talk to him and the girl with him. She made sure to start to apologize to the girl, but it ended up being his cousin, and she said it was hilarious to see someone even attempt to race him. He laughed at Kerry's erratic driving, saying she was crazy, which made her blush with pride, and an immediate friendship was formed. They drove out to a wooded spot, and the girls got into his four-wheel-drive and bounced through the woods, coincidentally being invited to an upcoming party. Kerry thoroughly enjoyed the ride in the woods, which made her miss her pickup; there was nothing like the feel of flying through the woods, dodging trees and rocks, and mainly killing any shocks that might have been left on the vehicle. Charlie ended up being the only guy where no phone numbers were exchanged for weeks, and the girls were treated as one of the guys, ending any worries about getting drunk with Charlie and his friends, and they began to hang out with his Montrose crew almost every day after that, and neither Charlie nor his friends ever tried anything with either of them.

They ended up finding some of the funniest, craziest parties in that stupid little town in some of the strangest ways. Making a wrong turn, having to ask for directions, and being led down a one-way back road that was mainly used for quads, only to find a huge bonfire deep into the woods, being invited to numerous graduation and birthday parties where they would only know two or three people at the beginning of the night, and never having to pay for a beer once. Then one day they were pulling out of the gas station in town (the only one that didn't care that people headed in after a party merely to use the bathroom, and rarely buying anything), and Kerry sort of cut in front of another car. This was prior to the night's party, and she hadn't been drinking yet, but she still didn't like the idea of someone tailing her, and she hadn't realized that car was going so quickly in a 25 mph zone, so she sped up a little bit, in an attempt at avoiding pissing off another driver. Even though most of their party spots were with strangers, sometimes the idea that there really were psychos out there crossed Kerry's mind, and she attempted to avoid stupid things when she was sober. Backfired this time, as they sped up too, and Kerry's first thought was, "You asshole. I'm trying to give you room," so she sped up some more. It was at this moment that the lights flickered on, and the unmarked cop car gave its indication for her to pull over, and Kerry assumed she was screwed. She pulled over, and he walked up to the car and asked if she knew what she was doing. Not if Kerry knew why she was being pulled over, just in general if she knew what she was doing. Kerry gave a pathetic sigh, told him about realizing too late she had pulled out when she shouldn't have, and explained she wasn't trying to speed, just that she was trying to give him more room, until he pulled her over. He just looked at her, probably trying to decide if she was lying or just that stupid, and said he'd be back. Luckily, Kerry had no speeding tickets or points, so he came up with a clear record on her license. He gave her a warning with the message "driving at unsafe speeds," which made both girls laugh uncontrollably as soon as the cop was gone, since she was going about 45 when he did pull her over. Which supposedly could be unsafe in a 25, but it wasn't exactly a dangerous road or anything, so they laughed about it. Kerry also thanked her lucky stars she wouldn't have to take a speeding ticket home. In order to read the ticket more carefully, they drove to a neighboring parking lot to read the ticket, and to laugh more about it without swerving all over the road, when some guy came up and asked if they had been naughty girls or what. He saw them getting pulled over, and Kerry decided to show him her first warning, proving her dangerous speed problem, getting pulled over going 45. He laughed with the girls about it, although not quite as giddily as they laughed about the unsafe speed, and invited them to a kegger. This was how it was in that town, and it was a safe town; nearly everybody knew everybody else, and almost nobody was crazy. They had a great time that night, watching people climb trees, only to fall out into piles of leaves that were disgustingly rotten and wet.

20

They were arrested with Charlie after about two months, and luckily ended up getting disorderly conducts instead of a wide variety of charges. Wait, an explanation is needed before vague details start flying around. The entire "crew" Kerry and Mary were with one hot summer evening decided to party in the woods, not only because it was a beautiful summer night, but because Charlie's parents told everyone to go away. So, they all drove out into the woods on a deserted old dirt road where they passed maybe two or three houses on a stretch of eight or more miles. It was beautiful out there, and the sounds of the night and of summer were the only ones around besides the drinking and carrying on of the party-goers. Cameron came out to see Kerry, but her friends made fun of him because he was being rude and ignorant, so he left. After a bit of fighting, of course. Then Kerry was upset, so Charlie and Luke (another of the crew) tried to make her feel better, giving her hugs, and telling her nice things about herself which made her question whether they wanted to keep their friendship just a friendship, but it was still nice to hear someone describe your beauty and your wonderful personality. But Kerry ended up not even feeling like drinking, not only because they had bought this truly nasty shit, but because of the summer sounds relaxing her and sleep calling her name, so she ended up only having like three. Then she found a fruity drink and drank it too, but other than that, she just wanted to be left alone. She wandered around the cars, roamed around the woods, always close enough to hear her friends, and then she finally got tired and headed to Luke's car to sit down, maybe fall asleep. That's when they saw the headlights, and they didn't come in slow motion like in the movies or on TV, they just appeared to, well, appear. Kerry glanced down to grab a cigarette out of her pack, looked up, and saw three police cars, lights on and everything. She slid the bottle of fruity stuff under the passenger seat she had been ready to fall asleep in after her cigarette, but instead found herself putting her hands up, because she saw Luke had his up. The cop came and opened the door for them all, and they all went and stood in front of the headlights of their cars. Mary and Kerry had to empty their pockets, while they put the few friends of theirs that were also under 21 in handcuffs. The three people who were over 21, they let go! Kerry was in disbelief! Their one buddy, who had bought the beer actually, was so drunk he could barely stand, and they let him drive away! Free! Charlie, on the other hand, had been peeing behind a tree when they pulled up, so he just kind of slid away. Although, the next day we found out he got lost in the woods, and although the cops showed up at midnight, he didn't get home until after four a.m., and he only lived about five miles away. They all laughed about that at poor Charlie's expense. But the cops had to wait until a female arrived, so she could pat the girls down, then handcuff them as well. They waited outside talking with the police and chain-smoking until she arrived, and then they were put in the back of the car to head to the station. They hoped being so nice to the police would give them an advantage when it came time to press charges (if any), but they weren't sure, and Kerry was still tired, so she just felt as if she were going through the motions of the arrest, instead of this being the first time. Instead of being panicky or worried, she was merely waiting for the next step, as if she knew this was coming, and was almost relieved that it finally happened, and she could get the mental help she knew she needed but would never ask for. The girls noticed the cops had the lights on but not the siren, so they both asked the cops to turn it on. They kind of laughed and asked why. Kerry told them she planned on this being the only time she was ever in a cop car and she wanted to make it good. He didn't turn the siren on, but at least he had a sense of humor and laughed some more. Kerry ended up not being able to say the same about her mother.

Angelica was woken up by that tiny township's cop at about three a.m., and since Kerry's car was still out in the woods, she also had to wake Uncle Wesley up. They were both very angry when they came to pick her up, but the good news was that she didn't get an underage drinking charge. She could have ended up with littering, public drunkenness, trespassing, disorderly conduct, drunken driving, and something else. Honestly, Kerry had stopped listening after she realized he could come up with as many as he wanted to. But they gave Mary and Angelica the mug shots they had taken of the girls (To scare them? To keep them from doing this again?) and a disorderly conduct. They said it was a smaller fine. Kerry thanked God that's all she got though; if that was the smaller fine, she'd have been totally screwed with the other one(s). They each ended up with a $225.50 fine, which neither of them could afford, so they had to make payments. Which is sad, because every month it reminded them that they weren't as good as they thought, considering they finally got caught. At least they got a ride home though, and didn't have to wander around the woods at four a.m. like Charlie had to!

21

That was when Cameron started picking fights with Kerry, his reasons being because he thought they were getting too close and hanging out too much. He didn't want a girlfriend, he just wanted a playmate. Kerry's mind reeled at this, as they had never even come close to sex, and she was still convinced it was her appearance that was deterring him. They did act like a typical high-school couple, together all the time, kissing, and there was touching, but it was never taken any farther. Kerry always thought they would become a couple so eventually it would go that far, but there was no hurry because he would still be there, right? Around this time, Kerry started smoking marijuana regularly, wishing she had a fairy godmother. She would smoke and drink not for fun, but to feel less depressed, and always wanted more. Writing was the only thing she actually truly liked to do, and at this time all she did was write random things after she had gotten high. Usually diary entries riddled with memories of Calvin's touch, so horribly engrained on her skin, on her back, on her lips. Every time the images scrambled across her mind, she became ill, and her body began to shake, and she was so afraid. She wasn't sure what she was afraid of, but she would hide the writing, the pens, and the notebooks, and she would dig out her Beggar Box. This was what she called the box she used to keep her weed, her pipe, her cigarettes, incense, and pictures. She would become afraid to write at all at this high, worrying constantly that she would push herself to write, and instead of it being the only thing she loved to do, the only outlet she allowed to release the inner angst and turmoil screaming through her mind, she was afraid she would drive herself to hate writing, and therefore have no outlet at all to rid herself of her memories. At these times, in a drunken high where everything was spinning, the colors were streaming together, and Calvin's hands were everywhere, she would grab Daddy Bear, a picture out of the Begger Box of her and Pappy, and she would curl up on her bed and cry. Although no tears would come, it felt like she was empty, laying there weightless, wondering where the world had gone, and why it had left her with Calvin's hands everywhere. She couldn't escape them, they were surrounding her, and she would fall asleep with a death grip on Daddy Bear. Upon waking, her eyelids would be swollen, because she found at night she could cry, and it was only then that her mind would allow the tears to release, and her pillow would be damp with the salty mixture that had seeped from her eyes throughout the night.

Little in life made her happy or free, and these nights had been occurring too often, driving her mad. Which was why she went out partying with Mary every opportunity she got. Kerry was now afraid of Cameron also, because he made her smile and laugh, when she knew in the back of her mind that the other choice was curling up with Daddy Bear, smoking a joint alone, and wondering when the hands would return. She had never had that feeling of happiness that Cameron gave her, and didn't know what to do with it. Despite this, he left her alone before she even realized that he was all she had wanted her whole life. Well, that's not entirely true, it wasn't him she wanted, but the concept of him. She had put this idea of him into her head, and that is what she wanted, not how he acted, but the dream of him she had in her head of how she could some day see him acting. The dream of the guy he would be after he knew about the hands, and he would hold her in his arms, blocking all chance that the hands would get to her. He would understand her pain, he would mix her drinks, and he would roll her joints. She was wrong in that assumption because he never liked her (or so he said ever so passionately, and every time they spoke now), but she thought she missed her opportunity at happiness. Part of her wanted to believe she had missed it so she could just fall completely into the spell the depression had over her. It would give her an excuse to spend her paychecks on liquor and weed, give her a reason to be trying to find other highs.

22

    Kerry was desperately trying to snatch Cameron's attention at this point, but he was starting to hang out with another girl, similar to how he had hung out with her when they first met, so eventually she assumed she was being replaced. Except he was rude when she called and he was with her; he would make it a point to tell me something like, "I told you to stop calling, and NO we can't hang out tonight."
    It confused Kerry, especially when she hadn't asked him to hang out, but she decided she had been replaced, had been eliminated, and had been told to hit the road. She wasn't sure what happened, she had done the "dating" thing with him, and had assumed the next part would be deciding they were an actual couple and having sex, but she was gone before she knew it. Out of the picture, before she even had a chance in the spotlight.
    So, what did she do, upon this final realization that she had been thrown away? She called Mary over, and they got drunk. They were Cameron-hating all night, taking shots at each thing they could think of that sucked about him, and by the time Kerry was completely toasted, she was angry also. So, she decided to go visit her hunny, and show him what it meant to hurt Kerry Lucille Ryler's feelings. Mary drove the two of them out the old brick road up to his house, and they drove past slowly, but trying not to be suspicious (probably didn't work since they were both drunk), and they parked down the road off to the side. They did their best at pulling the dark car into the trees off the road, but were also afraid of getting stuck on a rock or something, so they decided to just hurry on with their business. Kerry pulled the knife out of her pocket as she ran to his new car, his baby, with the brand

new paint job, the flame job down both sides, and the exhaust that would "make the neighbors want to kill me" and she jammed it into the expensive new low-profile tires he had just bought, pulling it so it would leave a gash. She knelt by the driver's side listening to the hiss of the air gushing out of the tires, and smiled. Mary was on the other side doing something, but Kerry couldn't tell what. Then simultaneously, they took off, running as fast as they could, hearts pounding, and jumped into the car, speeding away and hastily lighting cigarettes.

Mary told Kerry she just took the valve cap off her side, and she was shocked to hear that Kerry had actually slashed one of his new tires. That wasn't Kerry at all, not revenge, not anger, not vandalism! But she was furious, and sick and tired of people doing shit to her that she didn't deserve. Her hands were shaking, her blood pumping furiously through her veins, and as she pulled the tiny bottle of vodka out of the glove box that she had stashed for them, she hadn't felt more alive in her entire life. She had finally done what nobody expected, and all she really did was show him how much she cared, and he showed her the door! She was done with that!

He never even mentioned this to Kerry on the phone (not that he talked to her much anyway), so she never gave it a second though, after the next morning. Then, a month later, Mary got stood up and came over, and they got drunk again, man-bashing.

And they decided to go visit him again. Ready to go, Mary put a beer in her pocket (one for the road). Once they got there, Kerry with a sharper knife this time and the keys to her car, she giddily drove the key down the side of the flames, making little x's on the paint, and making the flames look as if they were being attacked, finishing it with a deep gash once again to the driver side tire. It made the same wonderful hissing noise as the air ran out immediately, but it was a lot louder this time (or they were either drunker or not as drunk), so once again they ran as fast as they could and rushed home to have more drinks, this time celebratory ones. On the way home, though, Kerry's cell phone rang. Her heart nearly stopped as the caller ID flashed

Cameron's name at her, and she was scared to answer it, because it was him, the caller ID said so as it flashed along with the rings, but if she didn't answer, then she'd definitely look guilty. She took a deep breath and coughed a little before she answered in a voice that portrayed she had been sleeping. They had turned the radio off, the windows were all up, and they were crawling along the road at a snail's pace, praying no cops saw them until they were off the phone. He asked where Kerry was, sounded really pissed off, and when her tired-sounding reply was that she was in bed, he said, "Whatever, bitch," and hung up.

She figured right there, that she had lost any chance that she had with him ever, so she downed many more once they got home, and smoked a whole lot more than planned.

23

Love is so awful when it is one-sided. When you wrap your heart up, put a bow and card on it, and give it to someone who tosses it in their closet, when you would do anything in the world to see them smile or hear them laugh. Why do I love him and why does my chest ache so? The tears flow, and I can't stop them. My eyes ache, my throat is raw, and I need a tissue. Even after I sleep, he's in my dreams, as well as my prayers. He's a constant thought running through my head. I want him to miss me and love me so much, but I can't make him do what he doesn't want to do. Pictures do not make an adequate reminder of how his brown eyes looked when he smiled, or how warm and safe a hug from him felt. And how relaxed and comfortable he looked as he slept with me in his arms. His smiles lit up his whole face, and were contagious, I couldn't be near him and I couldn't look at a picture of him without smiling. Sometimes, more recently, it's a smile of regret. What did I do wrong? Why did he move on? What does he see in her? Did I have it; was that what he saw in me? Did I lose it? Or did he take it when he left? I can't change the past, but I don't regret it either. I remember him, I remember the good stuff. I remember playing the neon game, his house, being quiet while we made out, watching movies, drinking lights, soft pack light cigarettes, him getting sick, his new car, the van, the graduation party, his best friend's party, boogerface, green candy, pop (warm, shaken, and flat), and a kiss. I remember the bad stuff, too, but the good stuff defines the reasons I still like him, so why say the bad?

24

Looking back, most of those "good" memories were really just friendship things. Stupid stuff when Kerry looked back and realized they were the reasons she liked him then. Oh well, she couldn't have everything.

One night, it happened! We kissed!
But, alas, then I woke up, pissed.
Just friends, growing closer every day.
My heart would stop when you looked my way.
Everyone thought we were one.
But you'd never be so dumb.
I'm not the prettiest color of crayon.
And I'm probably so boring you'd yawn.
Now you are one with another.
I'm smart, I knew not to bother.
Except my one lacks a hon.
You've got your chick
And what do I get?
I get to spill my fears,
My heart, my tears.
To no one, for I am alone, solo
Because I've got no place to go.

25

Kerry's luck started to go downhill soon after Cameron's exit. She was pulled over again shortly after this. She had been driving 80 in a 65 mph zone, and she got caught. She was given a ticket, but the cop wrote that it was failure to obey a traffic device, so she didn't get any points. She still had to pay a fine, in addition to the one she was still paying on for getting caught in the woods, but at least it was a different magistrate's office, and it was cheaper than a regular speeding ticket. She was just glad she hadn't gotten any points yet; she could barely afford the car insurance bill she had now, especially after the wreck, and especially between trying to pay for her outings with Mary while working part-time at the mall. Imagine with adding tickets onto it, no way. She can't add another bill to her mother. Angelica was pissy enough when she got the other fine. Kerry felt like a huge disappointment to her because she kept doing stupid shit and getting caught. At the same time, she kept doing them, kept drinking, kept smoking, and kept hanging around with the wrong people, tempting fate that she would eventually pick the wrong crowd and end up getting raped or killed. At least she had her job now; she had started working at an adult toy store (not sex toys, well, not ONLY sex toys); it had fun stuff for everyone, and everything was something funny or crazy, plus it was right by the local college, so all the cute college guys came in. With everybody sort of drifting away from each other, she had to start something that would keep her busy. Mary and her still hung out, but Mary started at a college two hours away, and Kerry had chosen a local one, for a lot of the wrong reasons, but in essence the paperwork was completed, and it was set in stone that she stay there for at least the semester she had applied for. She didn't go to their little town as much without Mary, because it just wasn't as fun. Most of the guys had started moving away, or getting better jobs, or starting college too, so there wasn't as much to do anyway. Plus, it was getting cold, so no partying outside anyway. And Cameron was pretty adamant when he decided he wanted as far away from Kerry as possible, and he hadn't been answering her calls, so she stopped calling him. She decided she might be desperate and pathetic, but she wasn't stupid. Plus, she was partly afraid if she started talking to him, she might stupidly apologize for vandalizing his stupid car.

26

With Cameron out of the picture, Kerry focused on her work. Which, in turn, made her focus on Aiden. She met him while working, and he said he was attending a wrestling match at the college she was attending, so she assumed it was a college match. He was staying with a friend there, so she went to visit him. He kissed her and held her, and they talked and had a fun time just being together. She found out he lived about two hours away from her though, and that he wasn't in college. He was actually three years younger than her, which freaked her out horribly. Was that considered statutory rape? How had she kissed someone that much younger than her? And why was she making plans to go visit him? He liked her as much as she was enjoying being with him, but when his parents found out how old she was, they wanted the two to be with friends when they hung out, and were never allowed to be alone. She wasn't falling for him though, even though he expressed interest in her. So that's a good thing, it's a start, right? (Even if she was sort of falling for him, but refused to admit it to herself.) She truly believed that she only wanted to be around him, because it was a "bad" thing. Her heart told her that was a complete lie, because she wouldn't call him as often as she did if it was "bad," she would just visit him more. But his parents said it wasn't allowed, and he was younger than she was, although he looked at least 19; it was a definite challenge not to fall for his sexy hazel eyes and very muscular body. She definitely wanted what she couldn't have. Anyway, despite the rules, they hung out a few times and acted like madly in love schoolchildren when they were together. They even planned a few visits where his parents wouldn't be home, and had sex the one day when they were alone at his house. And he was a virgin, and it was the best Kerry had encountered in her short sex life so far. She visited Aiden a few times, and on the way home two of the times, she got two speeding tickets. Points and everything, nice little fines to pay, and anger from Mommy. Both were 80 in a 65, and she now had four points, of the few she was allowed by the state. And she owed another two hundred bucks, one ticket was $70, and the other was $130.50. Aiden wasn't making her depression any better; he was only giving her happy spurts and speeding tickets. There seemed to be no end to this madness.

Did she like Aiden so much because in her mind she knew they'd never be able to be together? He did make her feel sexy, beautiful, and liked (not loved), and she really enjoyed being around him, and she drug Belle out to Aiden's home in Raleigh for double-dates with her and one of his friends. The double-dates were the occasions she visited where his parents knew. She had gone a few days where they weren't home so they could have sex again. She had to get away from all of this. She was so depressed, turning to Aiden and putting a lot of pressure on him to make her smile or make her laugh. Kerry knew if he realized what she was doing and the random horrendous thoughts running through her mind constantly, he'd run. He had no idea that she could have gotten into a lot more trouble than just a few speeding tickets if the police would have seen her blood-shot eyes, and noted them for what they were instead of believing that she was just tired. She was high and drunk each time, but since she had been this way all the time lately, nobody seemed to realize the change, except for Angelica, and she was engrossed in her own pill-popping depression that she had no room for Kerry's mind-numbing behavior. The only way she would have noticed Kerry's actions was if she would have actually counted her pills and noticed that the painkillers were dwindling in number.

27

    After all the confusion and relentless depression, Angelica finally offered Kerry to go on a vacation during her spring break. Kerry decided to go visit Mark in Florida. Kerry thought she could finally relax and escape. Mark's friend, Ian, and Kerry had started talking online a few months before, and when he heard Kerry was coming down, he was ecstatic. Kerry was too, but not because she was going to meet him. Wait, that's not 100% true. That was a little bit of it, but with all that had been going on, Kerry just needed to get away. It just wasn't fair. Her biological father didn't call her or tell her to have fun, but that was probably because he hadn't even responded to her letter, and Kerry decided he had given up on her. Kerry figured she just had to leave. Then, she came down, met Ian, and caused more problems. He obviously was more into Kerry than she was him. He followed her around the first few days after she got there, and flirted incessantly with her. She was flattered, but refused to flirt back because in no way, shape or form was she getting into something when she was 17 hours from home. What kind of relationship would that lead to? She was on vacation, and although he was a true sweetheart, and he was very polite, and she got the distinct feeling he liked her, she couldn't let herself fall into another trap when she was still working on getting over Cameron and while she was trying not to fall in love with Aiden. After the one night Ian left Mark's house, Kerry found a note beside her bed.

    Kerry,
    I'm sorry if I acted like a jerk or a loser last night. I thought that we had grown close or at

least not distant after talking to each other online and on the phone; I shared things with you that I had not told other people. I really got to a point where I cared for you and your feelings. I was genuinely concerned for you when you were depressed. After you told me you were coming down here, that was all I could think about. I didn't want to get my hopes up too much but I did. I was so nervous on the drive to the airport and waiting for your plane to land. I was so worried that you wouldn't like me once you saw me. I didn't care what you looked like, I was just so happy to be around you. I do think that you are a beautiful and intelligent person. I really was wanting to spend time alone with you and I got really down when we didn't get the chance to do that the last two days; I wanted to be around you, but I didn't want you to think I was smothering you. Remember when I told you that I was becoming a very sensitive person? I am totally depressed now. I really want to be around you and spend time with you and I don't feel the same from you. I don't know if you do like me and are afraid to tell me, or if you don't like me; please tell me if you don't so I can get that illusion out of my head and my heart. My heart feels really heavy right now, my ears are hot, and I can't eat. I'm sorry to ramble, but I just wanted you to know what I was thinking*

Ian

Kerry was horrified. She couldn't believe she finally had someone in love with her, and it wasn't any of the men she had fallen for. Kerry felt like she should do to him what Cameron did to her, just because that is how the story of her first love came about. She felt bad for him, but mostly she decided she was just angry. This was supposed to be her vacation and she tried to leave all her problems in North Carolina! She didn't know what to tell Ian. She just wanted to hit him, slap him across the face and make him understand how truly moronic it would be to start any kind of relationship while she was there. She only had four days left, and she was not spending them with, sort of, a stranger. She wanted to visit Mark and his friends, party, and not worry about anything while she does down there! She didn't come there to fall in love, and she had told him online how she felt towards love anyway. It's so stupid and pointless. What good has it ever done anyone? Happiness isn't forever, and neither is love. She really didn't have time to listen to the virgin boy's feelings any more than she had to worry about world peace. She didn't understand how he could love her without knowing her. She loved Cameron, because she used to know things about him no one else knew. His expression in his sleep, the lies he told (until she found out he was telling them to her), the foods he ate, the cigarettes he smoked, that kind of shit. She truly believed he was being honest and genuine with her for a long time. That shows the beginning of how stupidly gullible she was. Ian had so many heartbreaks ahead of him it wasn't even funny. Kerry was sure she would get yet another when she returned, because she thought for sure she was lying to herself about Aiden, and she knew she was falling for him, and doing it quickly.

Why?
We kissed, we cuddled, we held each other.
To you it was magical, to me, it was fun.
I wasn't popular, wasn't cool.
It was always just me, just one.
When you held me though, it was different, better.
But it was temporary, you had to go.

LIVING AS A MISTAKE

You'd return you said, I thought never.
But, alas, you did, and within weeks.
Then it hit, you thought we were an item.
Confused, I ran. I was meek.
Shy, me? Not usually, just with men.
They kept their distance, usually.
I assumed you were a fluke.
I thought you were acting cruelly.
I assumed it was to hurt me, a mean joke.
I was wrong, and I hurt you.
It hurt me still.
I ran so you couldn't break my heart, too.
Like the few others I wanted to kill.
I'm sorry, I was wrong.
But I can't change the past.
I don't regret my decisions after long.
In my mind I know, guys don't last.

28

Everything confuses me. Life, school, love. Is there truly a point to life? If so, what is it? Do we ever find out in our lifetime? I don't understand emotions either. Why do they pop up so unexpectedly? I had a good day today, but now I feel like giving up everything no matter what the consequences. I hate feeling this way, but nothing seems to make it go away. I'm afraid of life, so very afraid. I hate trying for anything, I'm so afraid of failure. Which seems to be following me around lately. I can't do college. It isn't working out at all the way I'd planned. Five years ago, I had major plans for what I would be when I was where I am now. I'm nowhere near that spot and my ladder doesn't seem to go that high. I need to waste away, disappear. At times like this, I feel as if nobody would notice. And yet I know I would leave a few really hurt people. Notice I said a few. Mary would miss me, but she has her new boyfriend now, and with work, her own studies, and babysitting him, she is so busy I doubt she'd have time to mourn. My other friends are so busy with their lives, they barely notice what I do now as it is. My mom would be the worst. I'm almost her whole life. And I love her, but sometimes I wish more for her. I'm sure she has hopes and dreams left unfulfilled. I doubt she had childhood dreams of being a single mother working full-time just to make ends meet at the local magistrate, typing up fines for speeders. She is my hero though, truly. She is so strong-willed and proud that I doubt I could lead even her life, even if I doused myself in drugs, drinking, and pills as she does now. As of now, I'm having a hard enough time leading my own life.

LIVING AS A MISTAKE

The really sad thing is that most people get upset after something big happens to them. Nothing happened to me today. I yearned for something to, something awful, maybe somebody would wreck into me, yell at me, or call me a rude name, anything to be depressed about. Nothing significant happened to me today, though. Maybe that is the problem. Nothing. If something would happen, maybe I'd be happy. When I see a star, that's what I wish for. Not money, not a car, not a mansion. Happiness. Plain and simple. Winning $1 on a scratch off lottery ticket would make me happy. A phone call from someone who asked for my number. Although nobody has done that recently, so that won't happen either. I doubt Cameron will suddenly want to chat with me. Maybe what's wrong with me are the images that keep running through my mind. I wouldn't mind hearing from Aiden either, but since his parents pretty much implied we'll never be together, and he stopped calling too, I just have yet another heartbreak from him. My imagination working overtime, seeing me being a single mother on welfare desperately trying to make ends meet. Almost twenty. I had such plans. Where did I go wrong? I'm going to fail college, but do I go back? I wanted to be on the dean's list, I wanted the Pulitzer Prize, and I wanted to be a great writer. I'm not shit. I'll never be shit, and I'll never find somebody who'll care for me and protect me. Not that I deserve it anyway. What have I ever done that there wasn't something in it for me? I only hope that someday I'll be the person I always dreamed of.

29

Mary invited Kerry to go to her college for a weekend. Kerry had gotten prescribed depression medication on her last doctor's visit, and she wanted to have one last awesome party before she started trying to fix her head. The girls had a great time, met some new people, and learned some new games. It was sort of like their little town, in that the guys treated them as one of the guys. Kerry loved that, because then she was able to make fun of the girls that were all prettier than her. They drank all night, until the keg was kicked and the cigarettes were gone. The party had been off campus, barely though, so they had walked. They did the same to get home, except a little less gracefully. They were practically rolling down the hill, and laughing the whole way. Three guys from the party were escorting them though, because they were afraid they girls would get lost. Kerry was sure they thought they were going to get a "thank you" for walking them home, but since they just wanted some sleep, Kerry wasn't worried. Kerry noticed a campus police car when they were walking back to Mary's car (no, they weren't going to drive, they had more cigarette's there), so they quieted down, as not to attract attention. But where Mary had parked, there was a fence blocking the quick way to the dorm. So the guys helped them, and they all jumped the fence, forgetting the campus police car. The campus police car, on the other hand, immediately noticed the fence-jumpers, and yelled for them to stop. Not likely when it came to the girls, and the guys must have agreed, because they all took off running. They ran into the first doors after the guys. The guys ran faster, so Kerry immediately lost them inside the building, so she turned in the first door she saw, and Mary kept going down the hall.

LIVING AS A MISTAKE

Trying to confuse the rent-a-cops. Turned out Kerry's decision had been a bad one though, and the cop followed her into the men's room, where she had tried to take cover. She knew she was screwed when she saw the urinals lining the walls. Mary had run in the first open door, and into some guy's dorm room. He turned her in. So they were screwed. The campus police officer took them to the car and drove them to the dorm where they admitted they were staying for the night, and the female rent-a-cop said if they were good the rest of the night, and if she didn't hear from them again, they'd be let off. But they were in the dorm room, where they were now restricted in a college neither of them attended, with a bunch of girls in the hall neither of them knew. Mary had gone there last semester, but she didn't anymore, and her friend was living in a different dorm. So they were stuck. The girls down the hall, for some reason, wanted to mess with the two little drunk girls. They almost got into a fight, but it turned out to be just a screaming match, because those girls wouldn't stand behind what they were saying, and Mary and Kerry just laid in the campus room under their blankets yelling back. Well, somebody complained that the drunk girls in the dorm were being too loud, so they called the campus police back. And they hauled the girls off to the infirmary and got the phone numbers of their parents off of them, because nobody wanted to have the girls there. The good news was the rent-a-cops hadn't threatened them with any charges, just calling their parents. So, at one o'clock in the morning, Angelica had to call one of her friends, waking them up (somebody had to drive Mary's car home), and then drive two and a half hours to pick them up. Angelica was pissed. And she didn't know where this college was, so she had to call back a bunch of times and ask for directions. Kerry felt the world was caving in. Mary sat there and was a horrible prisoner, back talking and being a true little teenage smart ass, and she was upsetting Kerry and the rent-a-cop. You be nice to the cops, and you get out of a lot more; if you're an asshole, you deserve to get every charge they could give you. Kerry started crying, and was moaning about how stupid Mary was, how miserable her life was, and how she wished she had taken her medication before she came out, because she felt she needed it more now than ever. Kerry was still crying when her mother showed up, because instead of letting it go, she called everyone she could think of who would answer a phone at three a.m. Kerry sat in silence and answered as few questions as possible when her mother picked her up and they started home.

A few days later, they got letters in the mail from the on-campus police, who were citing them for disorderly conduct, public drunkenness, and purchasing alcoholic beverages as a minor. It was over...finally. They got caught, and there didn't seem to be any way out of this one. And they had to drive back to the college to go to the trial. They both pled not guilty, because the rent-a-cop hadn't tested them to see if there was proof of alcoholic intake at all, and there was no technical proof they had been drunk. Kerry felt so stupid though, and the depression medication hadn't started helping yet. This hole she was in just seemed to let the walls grow bigger. Not only did it seem she'd never get out, but she couldn't even peek over the walls now.

Mary's court date came first, and for some God-blessed reason, the officer never showed up for her. They drove two and a half hours to get away with it. Kerry couldn't believe it! Kerry's trial was a few months later, but to spare the suspense, it ended up the same. They got away with it; it had to be a miracle. Kerry decided to slow down after that. There were too many narrow escapes, and she still didn't know what she wanted to do in life, but she knew if she had something on her record, it would limit where she could go and what she could achieve. Not that she was achieving much at college now, but at least she was trying. Well, sort of trying, in between the pot and drunken episodes that she dreamed of and hid from the world during. She was still having the nightmares about the hands and still smoking just as much as she had been previously.

30

    The years passed with no contact at all between Kerry and Calvin. Kerry grew to accept she'd never see him or talk to him every again. That didn't bother her, it suited her just fine. She decided she could live the rest of her life not having spoken to him once and feel as if she hadn't missed a thing. As for her love life, or lack thereof, she dated on and off, but never anything serious, and nobody worth her time and, according to her, she wasn't worth anybody's time. None of them stuck around after they got to know her for about a week, and if they ended up having sex, then they stopped calling the next day. She ended up realizing that she thought that was what she wanted to do, appease them with sex. She also decided in order to rid herself of the horrid hands dreams, she would decide it was okay to have sex with them so soon after meeting them because it was *her* decision. That way, there was no chance of being talked into it, because she usually started them onto it. This was so wrong. Maybe it was because of Calvin forcing himself on her, and she just wanted to give her body to these guys she liked because it was, in the end, *her* choice. She couldn't blame anyone but herself, and that was a relief, because she wasn't anybody's victim. As for the "boyfriends," she wasn't even sure what her type was, not having known anybody other than the assholes who treated her like shit. The only male figures she had in her life were her uncles, who were single, and her male friends, who weren't really the type she would end up wanting to commit herself to anyway for a long relationship. They were the type who were awesome as friends, as long as they realized you always wanted to be treated as one of the guys and not one of the girls they used as one-night stands.

AMY ONDRIEZEK

All Kerry knew was that she hated her father for everything he'd done to her and everything he didn't do for her. She loved the fact that if anything ever happened, no matter what it was, she could always go back and blame him and the shitty childhood that he had caused. She wanted to tell him how much she hated him, and how much he ruined just by that stupid solo day where he introduced himself to her. She doubted it would have affected him had he ever heard how she really felt about him, he would have made up excuses and quickly tried to redeem himself, but she knew the truth. She would never love him ever in her life or even forgive him. What angered her though was when people said, "Well, I did it for love." She usually laughed at them, and practically scoffed at the idea, actually. Maybe it is because so many people say "I love you" and never realize what they are committing themselves to. How many people would honestly die for you after they have said they love you? There are only a select people Kerry decided she would give her life to save. She admitted to herself, Calvin was not one of them. She prayed for forgiveness for that as often as he ever crossed her mind, as well as praying for forgiveness for every hit of her joint, every shot of liquor, and every pill she popped. She did not believe Calvin had ever loved her, although she used to, but she did not anymore. Sometimes she believed she loved him, but at the same time, she truly wished a severe pain upon him so he could understand what she had gone through just being his flesh and blood. At the same time she thought she loved him, she also despised him with a true passion. He fed it himself. With the gifts he used to give her that Angelica paid for and wrapped, the cards he didn't seem to put any time into (how long does it take to sign "Love, Dad" anyway?), and the calls he forgot to make on important days. There were about 120 people in Kerry's graduating class, and probably at least twice that in fathers and grandfathers at the ceremony, but not a single father figure cheered and clapped for Kerry. Her mother, grandmother, and Candie cheered her on. He sent her a card with a wrinkled twenty dollar bill in it. His

LIVING AS A MISTAKE

brother, Uncle Danny, gave her fifty, in person and with a hug, telling her how proud he was of her. She decided she didn't care about the money, because how could something she never had be important to her? That also led to the question of why did Calvin mean anything to her at all? She wasn't sure exactly what he meant to her, but she knew that even anger or hurt from a person meant that they were affecting you in some way. She never saw him anymore, never spoke to him, yet he was still hurting her, and affecting her life. The thought that he didn't love her didn't really bother her, but the hurt that he purposefully inflicted on someone he could just pretend didn't exist did. And lately, with all the extra pot and pills she had been dosing herself on, she felt as if she was completely worthless, and wondered that if she died, who would be at her funeral? It didn't even phase her that she was having more and more fantasies about her own death. She came to the conclusion Calvin wouldn't attend his youngest child's funeral, and that hurt her. She hated her life, herself, and wondered often why she was so unloved. All she had ever wanted in life was happiness, and when she would wish upon a star, which she still did every night, it was still all she asked for, just a little happiness. She had been happy when she was with Cameron. To this day, a piece of her heart still belonged to him. In retrospect, he had been very similar to her most hated biological father, though. He hurt her many times, too, and she ended up just going back for more. Cameron pretended to be her friend and sometimes lover, then never acted as a friend should or treated her as a human, much less a lover or friend. He was never there when she needed someone, and, like Calvin, did not return her love (when she thought she actually loved them both). She swore to herself she would not make the same mistake three times, though. She tried to give her heart to her biological father, who stepped on it after trying to rape it, and gave it back to her bruised and tattered, then she gave it to Cameron, who pretended he didn't get the mail that day. Return to sender. Well, to hell with everyone, it was her heart, and nobody was getting their hands on it from now on. She will kill it herself; nobody would ever get the chance to break it again. She was going to cover it in cement; cement cracks, but it is very hard to break, and easy to repair. She was worried she was never going to recover. This dull ache in her head and in her heard would never fade, would it? She would always hurt and allow herself to be hurt, wouldn't she? She supposed she was destined to be a moron her whole life.

31

    Despite the weed and pills she was using most of her paychecks for, she wasn't living totally without ambition. She aimed to continue to go to college, and graduate with a bachelor's in business administration. The college of her choice was great, the classes gave her new life, and the students were civil in the first college she had attended. She never made any close friends, although she did try, a little. She thrived and lived mostly for her creative writing course, and it gave her a little hope for her future. Her GPA was great, too, she almost made the dean's list, but she had to work at her job at the mall, and since it wasn't paying her college tuition (she couldn't pay tuition and get stoned on that measly paycheck), she got a second job at the mall, just for over the holidays. She was so happy when that job ended though; she used to go out to her car and sit there hiding with a joint and cry, watching the snow fall around her. She would pop a few painkillers and try to relax before going back from her tiny breaks. Her co-workers there made her feel very small and very stupid. The job wasn't exactly rocket science, and even the employees that had been there years didn't have any more knowledge than Kerry did. (How long did you have to work at a place to learn everything about the few winter coats she was selling anyway?) She was grateful the day that job ended, and celebrated with some new pills. But with it ended her college career at her school of choice. It was just too expensive. She transferred to a public college. Still close to home, but much cheaper. She soon found out why it was so cheap and why the students were so laid back. The student-to-teacher ratio made her previous school look like a private school fit for a celebrity. Although her social life flourished there, and it was much easier to keep up her addictions to the pills, weed, and alcohol, as there were parties aplenty, her GPA soon dropped down dramatically, and her depression raged. She was put on academic probation by the end of her first semester there, which made her even more depressed. She had gotten high honors her entire life, and she hadn't received an "F" ever until she started at that school. She couldn't take more than one semester there, and she left. She had actually stopped going to a few of the classes, because the teachers made her want to cry in class, and she still refused to cry in front of anyone, including her mother. She couldn't handle all the crap she was taking from everyone. So she gave up. She saw a trend developing; every time she started to fail at something, or it got too hard, she got stoned, held Daddy Bear, and quit at whatever it was that was hurting her ego.

32

The next person that made a difference and Kerry pushed farther into her still sinking depression was Chase. She met him while driving around with Mary. They had been looking for a party and he knew where one was. Kerry's living obsession was getting drunk and high now; it was her escape from reality. And Mary was always up to go out drinking. Kerry wasn't sure if she ever realized Kerry was becoming an addict, and was content just being a miserable alcoholic everybody pitied and nobody talked to, but she went with her anyway. Kerry would smoke it up alone, then go pick Mary up, and right before her first drink she would pop one or two painkillers.

They followed Chase to the beer that night, not caring where they were going, and once they got there, just hoping they'd be able to find their way home when they were drunk later. Chase flirted with Kerry all night, and although he wasn't very good looking, he flirted with HER, and that was new, so immediately she took a liking to him. Somebody yelled "COPS!" about four hours into the party, and since the campus episode, they both just took off. Angelica would kill Kerry if she had to be called again at three a.m. for her getting caught drinking again. She was already so pissed off that she was sneaking out to these parties when she was supposedly working. Kerry wasn't even sure whose house she was at, but she crawled under their back porch and hid behind the hot water heater. She watched Mary keep running and she heard her blue plastic coat make its "swish swish" noise. Kerry took the glow stick out of her mouth and buried it in the dirt so the cop wouldn't see it, and she snuffed out the cigarette she had, for fear the cop would see or smell it and find her. He walked past her a few times, and even stopped in front of her once, but never saw her. Her heart was pounding so loud and fast she was actually afraid they'd hear it (she was still drunk, remember?). All the other people there only knew the girls' first names (see? Told you it was a good idea to party with strangers), so they couldn't really tell on either of the girls, and they did try. The cop walked past the porch Kerry was hiding under again and he heard Mary's coat, and he had her in his little "circle of wrongdoers" within a minute. When he turned to chat with his fellow officer, and they went to look at the cars in the driveway, she took off again. The "swish swish swish" flew past Kerry, and although she was scared shitless, she had to bite her tongue and cover her mouth so they wouldn't hear her laugh. When the cops saw no little girl in a blue plastic coat, they got pissed. They were threatening both girls, yelling loud enough for Mary, and Kerry was close enough to him that she could hear every word the cop said, but no one knew their names and the remaining drunken teenagers got into that much more trouble because of them. They had first names, and they assumed the green car belonged to one of the girls, but no one knew for sure. Chase was the only one knew for sure whose car it was, and he was still trying to "get some" from Kerry, so he remained mum on the subject. From previous party experiences, Kerry was glad this was the way they did things now. The only problem was that it was *Angelica's* car outside this guy's house. Both of the girl's IDs were in it, but Kerry (Thank God) locked her car everywhere they went. The police officer kept threatening he would find them, but Kerry figured if he did, she'd deal with that when it happened. She wasn't giving up. After the cops left, Kerry was afraid to move. The guys were walking around the house yelling for them that they had left, but she didn't trust them, not anymore. Chase kept walking around yelling for Kerry after the rest of them had stopped, and she wouldn't answer even him. She had overheard the cops say they'd just catch the little green car when it drove past them, but Kerry noticed they didn't pass the side of the house she could see, so they'd go that way. She didn't know where it went, but she wasn't risking getting caught driving drunk either. She doubted Mary knew where it went either, but they were always up for adventure, so it didn't really matter. Kerry snuck out of her hole covered in dirt and cobwebs, starting to feel a little sick to her stomach. She lit up a cigarette (which was a little bent from her laying on it) and lurked around the side of the house, whispering for Mary. After almost ten minutes, she crawled out of a rather rude looking thorn bush. She was all scratched up, and Kerry giggled as she started bitching about the cop. Kerry admitted she had seen her run past and she laughed. They agreed it was time to leave, and they were going do to it without saying goodbye just when Chase found them. He convinced them to stay until he felt the cop would have given up. Kerry agreed only if they could stay inside the house. Cops can't come inside. They're like vampires; you have to invite them in first. After Chase sweet-talked Kerry for a while, they decided to leave. Chase gave Kerry a good-bye kiss, and then they got into the car. It took them almost two hours to get the typical twenty minutes to her house, where the lights were all off, thank goodness. And after they drove around to avoid the cops, it turned out to be a big circle and they actually passed the party again. They were shocked and could barely believe it. What are those chances? The next morning, the phone woke Kerry up at eight a.m. It was the police officer from last night. He asked what the green car was doing at that guy's house (Kerry told him her mother wasn't home in order to avoid waking Angelica from her sleeping-pill-induced sleep), and she calmly stated that she had run out of gas and had gotten a ride to a friend's house and picked up the car later that night. Kerry knew he didn't believe a word out of her mouth, but he really had no choice so that ended up falling apart for him. Which worked for Kerry! The girls went out again that night, and somehow Chase found them again. Kerry had mixed feelings about that. He was nice and all, but men were trouble. They began hanging out nonetheless, and about a week later, he was her boyfriend. It was the closest thing to a serious relationship she'd ever had. He was nice to her and treated her decently, so she liked him. After about a month, he mentioned he would like having a cell phone because he was always working and couldn't get a hold of Kerry on her cell. He convinced Kerry it was for her as well as for him, but he had to get it on her account because he had bad credit. Before she realized it, she was becoming her mother, buying worthless men shit they didn't deserve. Kerry kept telling herself not to worry about him not paying because he had a job, but she started to worry when he never gave her money. He said to give him a month. Then they started fighting on a daily basis. Kerry never took the phone off of him, which turned out to be a big mistake. She was gullible, just like her mommy, and she was blind to what was happening right in front of her face. Kerry was being had. But she stuck it out as things got worse (she later guessed it was the depression, the more she had to worry about, the worse she could be). It was beginning to add up as another bill arrived, and she hadn't seen a dime from him. Then, they got into the biggest fight yet, and they broke up. This turned into a violent matter, and as Kerry was fighting for this worthless relationship in the driveway of his house, he shoved her into her car. She hit it hard, and fell onto the gravel, skinning her elbow and hitting her head on the driver's side door. He roughly grabbed her arms and yanked her up, telling her it was her fault for that, because she was yelling at him. Then he said it was over, and he apologized for hitting her, although his apologies were filled with "but it *was* your fault, you know."

Kerry was very upset and since she was on a medication for depression already, her doctor nearly doubled the dosage. She hadn't loved Chase, and she really wasn't even sexually attracted to him (which was partly the lack of forced sex they had), so she don't know why she got upset. She supposed it was because she knew he would treat her like shit, and then she could show herself she had an excuse to be so depressed and to hate herself. She smoked more for a few days; then another few days after that, they got back together, but that was short-lived. He gave her the usual guilt-trip and forcibly touched her (which gave her flashbacks about Calvin's hands), and she usually went numb over her whole body until he was getting up to throw the condom away. And if she raised her voice or yelled at him, or asked him for her money for the phone bill, he ended up shoving her or slapping her. This was how he silenced her, and she knew she was only staying as if to prove the relationship could work out. But he broke up with her again after a few more days, and about a week after that she found out he had been cheating on her with his friend. Kerry took that worse than the beatings and the sex, the lies. Not taking it well influenced her doctor to add another pill for anxiety and depression. Even then, Kerry let Chase use his phone. They decided to stay friends, and he promised he'd still pay her. Kerry believed him and told herself she would stop being friends with him once his bill was paid up, then she'd call and have the number cancelled. After the third and fourth bill had come and gone, she called and cancelled his phone, saying it was stolen. His total bill had peaked to four hundred dollars that Kerry didn't have. So, she went out to retrieve her property. He was at a restaurant, and she went there, already having called the police and asked their assistance. Kerry had no proof the phone was in his possession, so they wouldn't help. She was kicked out of the restaurant because she was loud and upset, so she was removed from the premises, without the phone. One of his friends called her the next day and asked her where she could meet him so she could get her phone. She told him to bring it to her at work, and she made sure mall security was there in case he said anything. After she got her phone, Chase, his new girlfriend, and all his friends started calling both cell phones from blocked numbers. They would call her names, hang up on her, and leave obscene messages. Once, one of his friends actually saw Kerry when she was driving around, and followed her. She made strange turns, turned around down a dead-end street, and he was still behind her. While she was driving, she called the police (grateful she had left her pipe at home), gave them his name and his car's description, and they went after him. Kerry met him and the police officer in a parking lot, and the cop made him apologize and promise to leave her alone. She was ordered to call the police back if he ever bothered her again. The girlfriend was the biggest problem though; she would call Kerry screaming (long after Kerry left them alone), and she'd threaten to find Kerry and beat her up. Kerry wasn't even sure what she had done; she was told he had been cheating; she accepted reality as much as possible and stopped calling him; all she wanted after that was the cell phone. Which she now had, and she didn't have any phone numbers to any of them as he had deleted his phone book, so she left them all alone. She even stopped going to the same places, for fear she'd see them. Do not get her avoidance of them wrong, she was definitely not afraid the tub of shit's girlfriend was going to beat her up. Kerry actually hoped she would, because then she could get pain medication as well as the depression medication, and for once she wouldn't have to pay for the meds. Out with alcohol; take as many free happy pills as possible! At this point in her life, Kerry was very depressed, and she was really thinning out, which made it funny the tub of shit's girlfriend often called her fat, and Kerry wondered why she couldn't have been depressed when she was in high school trying to lose weight. Kerry was now thinner than Chase's new girlfriend too, and she had lost fifteen pounds in the last week. She was still convinced she'd never be happy, and she'd never find the right guy, that she'd be stuck in the kind of relationship Angelica had been stuck with. Kerry swore she'd kill herself first.

33

What the hell is wrong with me?? Do I do this to myself? Why!? All I want is a drink, that's all, just one little drink, is that too much to ask? Why can't I be 21, so that I can just go out, buy myself a case, and drive drunk until God sees fit to take me into a tree so I can be with him, protected, unable to be harmed up there with him? I want to take some pills; make this shit go away, take some Prozac, some Advil, have a fifth, maybe it'll all go away. Maybe. I can't even cry, I'm so hurt, and in so much pain, my stomach hurts, my head aches, I'm dizzy, and I can't do a damn thing about it! Why not!? My life sucks. I can't believe I'm still suffering through it after all these threats that I'll die. Maybe someday I'll understand this illness, but until then, I think it's a mystery as to why I'm so sick. Not physically sick, but mentally. I listen to sad songs that just make it worse, but I can't stop myself. I just want it to get so bad I'll just fade away into the darkness. Looking around I see that I've changed my surroundings so that I can be alone in times like this, but I haven't changed the fact that I can do nothing about this. I don't know what to do! I just want to sleep all the time, then I can't be upset. I will have dreams of a happy life and there isn't anything anyone can do to take that away from me. I will never find anyone who will love me while I'm this sick. All I do is enforce negativity, just like Chase said I did. I make my life a living hell and I do it on purpose. Why? I hate myself, but I do it every day over and over again.

AMY ONDRIEZEK

*fade...fade...fade...
nope still here.
damn*

Is there anyone who will ever die for me? Do I have a soul mate, someone to love me and care for me and baby me for all eternity? Someone to make me smile when the world is my enemy? Someone to stare at me like it was the last time they'd ever see me, and hold me like I was dying? I need a hero. I think I'm avoiding the world, but maybe it's avoiding me. I never go out to see or to have it prove me wrong, but that is probably the case. I say I hide from it, but it's hiding from me. It's as scared of me as I am of it.

34

From all the depression and the anger rising to the surface lately, Kerry had started taking it out on Angelica. She absolutely hated taking all her anger, rage and depression out on the one person who was always there for her, no matter what, but every time Angelica said one word, it was like she called Kerry a horrible name. Every time she saw her mother take a pill or mix a drink, fireworks of anger skyrocketed out of her mouth, aimed at her mother. She would just end up exploding on her for no reason whatsoever. Kerry couldn't take it. Her mother was the one person who was there for her sober and drunk, who loved her, and who cared for her no matter what she did in her life. She was even supportive, yet disappointed, at the fines Kerry had gotten over the years. Then again, since she was getting her own for drunk driving and abusing prescription medications, she wasn't exactly the proper role model. And yet it killed Kerry more than anything to fight with her, but at the same time she couldn't help it. So she decided her best bet was to move into a little apartment with her friend Candie. Kerry was still working at the mall on a supervisor's salary, so as long as it wasn't a crazy rent, she could handle it. And she'd been friends with Candie for years, so she knew with her working and Kerry working, they wouldn't get into each other's space. That worked fine; Kerry would have her own space, her own territory. She could be as miserable as she wanted, and only Candie would be there to see. If she happened to be home that day.

35

A few months later, though, Kerry started partying with Cole, a guy who worked beneath her at work. She had hoped new surroundings would make her a little happier. True, she wasn't fighting with her mom anymore, and she still saw her quite a bit, but now she was still miserable, *and* she had to pay rent, but at least she did try. On to Cole, though, she wasn't allowed to date him because she was his supervisor, so that made it exciting. But, allowed or not, he came to the apartment a couple of times to drink. He started calling Kerry every night, and they became quite close. They hadn't been working as much together because Kerry's boss had noticed them getting close, and she tried to stop it. But when they did get to work together, they goofed around, flirted, and Kerry felt all nice and gooey, because he gave *her* attention. He was cute, it was convenient to see him at work, and he acted like he liked Kerry. Sometimes that was enough for Kerry. Stupid reasons to like somebody, but that's how she had been lately. Just because they liked her, or even showed mild interest, she automatically liked them and made it into something it wasn't, so that when it fell through, she could be more depressed. So far, it had been working out perfectly like that. Kerry knew it was stupid and idiotic, but she couldn't seem to stop herself. She could only pray she could someday climb out of this misery she had fallen into.

36

Why can't I just tell him how I feel about him? Why does this scare me so? I only feel happy when I talk to him, and he doesn't know this. I want to tell him but I'm so afraid that he won't feel the same way about me. I'll scare him away like I did to everyone else. He wouldn't want to talk to me if he knew how completely psycho I was anyway. I'm going to let him off easy, because he won't ever feel anything for me anyway. Then it will be easier for me to get on with my life after this. I should not have had sex with him, because that just made me feel so much more for him, even though it wasn't very good. Sex is like glue for me though; no matter how bad it is, I want to believe it was special. Now I can't stop thinking about him, and I want him to know. But I can't tell him. I'm far too afraid to tell him anything. I doubt I will ever tell him, and he'll probably stop talking to me before he ever knows how much he means to me. It doesn't matter anyway, he praises me and tells me how pretty I am, but I don't believe a word out of his mouth. He's just another lying guy, so why do I feel this way? His girlfriend will probably make up with him, and he'll drop me because I probably am just an out until he's back on track with her. How cruel, you'd think I learned something from Chase. I guess I am just that gullible.

Surprise...surprise.

37

I'm waiting for Cole to call. I'm pathetic. He only acts like he likes me when nobody is around, or on the phone, where nobody can see who he is talking to. He has told me he just broke up with his girlfriend, and he thinks she just had a "spell" where she wanted some time away, and I have this sinking feeling that she'll come back just when I've really fallen (or THINK I've fallen) for him. He told me he might come visit me tonight, and I keep hoping out loud every time I light a cigarette that he'll call or somebody will knock. I know he has to see how much I like him. I just want to know how he feels about me. Even if he just wants to be friends, or doesn't want to talk to me at all. Why can't people be honest? Why can't they see the pain they inflict on others and just tell them the truth?

38

Well, I guess my happiness was short lived. Cole didn't show up. It's almost 2:30 A.M., and he still hasn't even called, so I guess it was not worth it after all. I can't believe I fell into that trap again! Will I never learn?? How many times do I have to be shown that no one will ever care about me or support me in my life?? A few more times? I hope not. I hope I never live to see the day where my heart gets broken again. I can't handle it. I'm having a hard enough time dealing with this and it isn't even a major deal. I have to go, I need a cigarette, and I want to cry in peace.

39

 I had this horrible dream, and when I woke up, I remembered it all. Cole never did call me, and I don't know if he's going to. But in my dream he said that he saw his girlfriend and they got really, really drunk together and ended up having sex. He said he was sorry, but he had to tell me. I can't remember if he said they were going to work things out or not, but even in my dream I couldn't cry. I was so upset today after I got my period and felt like shit anyway, that I took a bunch of headache pills. I have taken nine so far, and still can't sleep, but I'm dizzy now. He hasn't called so I'm afraid my dream was the truth. I still can't cry! I don't understand why, but it's making me worse. I took a razorblade today and cut across my arm. The immediate pain made me feel better, but it didn't make me cry either. I even reflected on that, and was relieved to feel the sharp razorblade as I slid it slowly across my inner wrist, feeling every second of the pain. I concentrated on the pain, trying desperately to relieve the pain in my head. Then I followed it with a large chug of vodka, enjoying the feel of the burn as it traveled down my throat. Now I have all these little cut marks, blood covered tissues, a buzz, and still no relief. I just want to feel better and I am not succeeding in this attempt. I feel like the end is close at hand, and it keeps taunting me but not taking me. I wish he would call me and tell me he didn't sleep with her. If he did, I'm afraid I might hurt myself even worse.

40

Well, I had a doctor's appointment today, actually two. The first one was with a shrink (of sorts). He asked me a bunch of questions, and I answered them, on the most part, very honestly. But I don't like the answers he gave me when I asked my share of questions. He said I was bi-polar, but not severe. I have Cyclothymiacs disorder, which he says is a very severe high and low period of moods. I am not sure I agree, and my aunt definitely does not agree. My Uncle Paul said that sounds sort of right though. I'm not going back to that doctor. I don't want to hear anything else he has to say about me. It'll just make me worse. It depressed me enough that there was a name for what I have. I thought I was just depressed. Guess I was wrong. On the way to my next doctor's appointment, I called Cole, I feel awful because I was depressed at work yesterday and took it out on him. Why!!! That's the only time I even see him now, as his calls became few and far between, and he hasn't come to the house since that last party weeks ago. And he when he does call, the conversation rarely lasts longer than a few minutes instead of the usual two hours. My only chance to convince him to like me is at work, and I was a horrible bitch to him! Condescending and arrogant, and just acting like my *boss! Which is horrible, trust me! I like him so damn much and yet I was treating him like shit, like I hated him, but I feel the exact opposite way. I don't understand why I do that, but it keeps pissing me off. Anyway, he forgave me and we're okay now. He said he wasn't mad at me, but I can't help but think that he was. He's just so sweet at work, he flirts with me and acts coy and subtle, then when there are no customers or watchful eyes judging, he'll touch my lower back or grab my leg. Something to let me know he's crushing, but then he acts like a retard when there's someone around. Guess he's just like the rest, trying to hide me, too embarrassed to let anyone know he thinks I'm pretty. I'm like the thing in the dungeon, nobody can admit it's there, but they love the hell out of it, and refuse to get rid of it. They just keep it there for when it's convenient. Anyway, once I got to my doctor's appointment with my regular doctor, I was preparing for my pap smear. Fun, fun. She said my cervix is inflamed, but I have to wait a week to find out if it's a problem. Everything else looked normal she said. Then she gave me a higher dosage of the newest depression medication, the one that was for anxiety as well. I don't know if I feel better or worse because of that. She also gave me a new pill, which is supposed to help the bi-polar part of me that the insane shrink told me I had. Not much to smile about with that on my head in any case. She gave me birth control too. So I should be having less severe menstrual cramps now. They just kick my ass; I needed something to ease that pain. Plus, with any luck, I'll start dating Cole and I will want to be on birth control. We already had sex once, and it wasn't that good, but if we date, I suppose I'll get used to him. We couldn't finish because neither one of us had any protection, but since he sucked, it didn't bother me. Oh I almost forgot, my doctor also said I have a lot of tenderness in my breasts. She said it's somewhat severe, but it doesn't mean increased chance of cancer. Which is good. Hope she knows her shit. I know it's early but I think I'm going to try to go to sleep. Cole's supposed to call later, so I hope I wake up to the phone ringing. By the way, those little scars I cut into my arm the other day are reminders of what I did. I feel no better, but now I can look at my arm and see I was worse, whether I feel better or not.*

41

OH my GOD!!! Yesterday was one of the worst days of my whole damn life. I was so stressed out at work. Then my boss reamed me out for being lazy and worthless (in a sense), but she also reassured me I was better than I was acting. She said I flirted too much, and had too many guys that came in just to talk to me. Which was ironic, because of all the guys that came in and flirted, was I dating? Or had anyone asked for my number? NO! This is getting ridiculous. Before I was depressed because nobody wanted to like me, now I'm getting in trouble at work for guys coming into the store and not liking me! Which didn't make me feel better. After she left though, it was a night of me and Cole working, which was rare since she knew I liked him too. Then Cole didn't show up for work though. I was so hurt. Even though I knew it didn't have anything to do with me, I blamed me. If he liked me he'd show up, right? Wrong! The world doesn't revolve around me! There is something wrong with me. I started that higher dosage of anxiety med I got and yesterday all I did was freak out, and today I'm dizzy and my hands are shaking really badly. I slept really well for a change though. Back to yesterday, the whole store was pissing me off, then everything angered me. Cole showed up with his shirt at ten 'til closing to get his paycheck and officially quit. Rita, a girl that works there and was called in to replace Cole, said the look on my face was great. I looked like I was going to kill him. I felt like killing him. But I think it's because I like him so much and I was just hurt. I got him his money, and he left. He called me last night and said he left quickly *because I had scared him. That's how mad I looked. I almost started crying when I was closing the drawers for no reason and Rita ended up calming me down. I can't believe I was so stressed out. I cheered up when Cole called me later and apologized, but even he had to talk to me for like an hour before I felt better. After all, it was his fault I was pissed anyway. Hopefully today will be better.*

42

Well, it's Monday, oh no, wait, it's Wednesday now, but anyway, on Monday I went to a tattoo parlor and got my tongue pierced. It didn't hurt like I worried for weeks about how badly it would. It's weird. I like it though. It didn't start hurting until about an hour ago, and even then it's just sore, not painful. Cole and I were speaking again; he hadn't called for about six days and I assumed the worst (typical me). But we were okay for two more days. Now he hasn't spoken to me since Saturday night. I don't think he's going to call me back. I might be overreacting again, but I really think he just dropped me, like he got amnesia and I am the only thing he doesn't remember. Oh well, I suppose I expected it, eventually.

43

It was the middle of December on that Monday that Kerry went to get her tongue pierced, and all of a sudden, Cole really did stop calling. She wasn't upset, she said it was coming after all. It nearly killed her he had quit work on a shift he was going to work with her, and she had to call in help an hour after he was supposed to start, because he was too wimpy to even call with a warning. And he also had that "ex"-girlfriend he was hiding Kerry from, so she wasn't relationship material anyway. A few days after he stopped talking to her, a (rare!) guy Kerry had given her number to while working actually called! He sounded sexy on the phone, and Kerry remembered him being very good looking. She also remembered that he lived near her apartment. So, when he asked if they could do something together, she jumped at the chance. There was no way she was waiting at home for Cole to call, and Matthew was here now. He was such a gentleman; he came and picked Kerry up at her mother's (she had been visiting), and he came to the door, knocked, the whole nine yards. He looked great, wearing a white visor over his sexy highlighted hair. They got into his car and left after he introduced himself to Angelica. They went to one of his buddies' houses, had a beer, and chatted. He introduced her to everyone, even the girl that was madly in love with him. They didn't tell her they were there on a date, but she later found out. He was nice enough that he didn't want to hurt her feelings even though he didn't like her the same way she liked him. So, instead of her thinking he was on a date, Kerry and Matthew convinced her that they were old friends, and Kerry was visiting. Since they got *very* serious *very* quickly, Kerry was sure she realized quickly they were lying, but she hoped the girl appreciated *how* they lied. Kerry found it so sweet, and so dramatically unlike her previous boyfriends. After they left the mini-party, they went back to Kerry's apartment and watched TV. After an hour of cartoons, he asked if he could take Kerry somewhere. She told Candie she'd be back, and if she disappeared, they would know who to look for. Kerry laughed at that though. Matthew was so incredibly sweet and sexy, and she wasn't worried about going anywhere with him. They got their coats on and got back into his car. He took her to the track field at his old high school. They walked out into the middle of the field, using his headlights to see, and being careful not to fall on the ice. They didn't say much, but it didn't feel uncomfortable, it felt right. Kerry was so scared she would fall for him. They looked at the stars, then decided it was too cold, so they turned to head back. They slipped and slid around on the ice, and when they were catching each other, they looked into each other's eyes. That was the best kiss Kerry had every experienced in her whole life; he was so gentle, and he tasted great. She felt so safe with his arms around her, and they walked back to the car together. Kerry's hands in his pocket, and his arm around her. It was scary how right it felt. Back at the apartment, they continued watching cartoons, and then a movie. He left later, around two or three a.m., even though he had work at like seven a.m. the next day. He said he'd call, and they'd hang out again tomorrow. The fact that Kerry believed him, and she had no doubt he really would call, frightened her terribly, and she wondered what she was getting herself into. She liked him so much already, and he was just perfect. As soon as he was out the door, Kerry nervously lit a cigarette, barged into Candie's room to wake her up, and asked her what she thought. Half asleep, she mumbled, "He's nice," and rolled over. Kerry did the movie pose that girls do when they're smitten, and she dreamily walked into the living room. Even if she never saw him again, at least she could live in the moment she had at that second.

44

The next day at work, Kerry saw the girl that was crushing on him, and she ran up to chat with Kerry. She was telling Kerry that since she was such good friends with Matthew, maybe she could put in a good word for her, because she liked him so much. Kerry smiled, said she'd do her best, then thought, *No way, girly; if he'll take me, I'm taking him!* When Kerry went into the back room for a cigarette break, she checked her cell phone and saw she had a missed call. It was Matthew! Kerry was shocked, because he actually DID call her back, and when she checked the message, he was talking about how much fun he had, and he hoped they could do it again tonight. The end of the message told her to just give him a call if she wanted him to come over. She wanted to call him right then and tell him to meet her at her door. But she didn't want to scare the poor guy either, so she just smiled and went back to work, praying for her shift to end quickly. About an hour later, this guy came up behind her and whispered in her ear, "Can you point me in the direction of the sex toys?" Kerry excitedly jumped up at the sound of that sexy voice, and said, "Let me show you the way," grabbing Matthew's arm to lead him over. He said he'd meet her at her apartment after work, and she hurried home that night. And, in fact, every night she worked thereafter, because after a week, he had an apartment key. That way, if Candie was working, he didn't have to wait until one of them got home. It was so great to be able to go home and have him there, arms wide open to hold her after a rough day at work. They had sex (mutual decision, not like Chase's guilty/forceful sex) a few days after they started dating, and he was so incredible. Kerry was amazed at how much she had been missing out on! She had known Cole and Chase were pretty bad, but now they were like, well, nothing at all. Matthew made her feel special, and not like "just a lay." She felt warm, and he finished the job he started. She couldn't believe that with the previous sex she had that she had never had an orgasm! She had thought she did, but Matthew proved her wrong. Kerry felt loved already. What was she getting herself into this time?

45

For the next few weeks, he'd call Kerry's cell phone, knowing she was at work, just so he could leave sweet little messages for her to get. She met his parents at Matthew's home a week after they met and decided they were a couple, and the meeting went well. Kerry was petrified they wouldn't like her, but they joked around with her, and she immediately fell in love with them. And his dad was a model of what she had envisioned her father to be prior to meeting him, down to the good-bye hug he gave her and his son.

Kerry hid all of her previous horror stories, including her nightmares of Calvin's hands, Chase's forceful sex, her mental anxiety, and her drinking problem. She only shared her love of weed with him, but he wasn't a pothead, and he was trying to help her quit by monitoring how much she smoked. She wasn't angry or vengeful with this new monitoring system, but she was grateful somebody cared enough about her to want her to be healthier. They spent all of their free time together, and even with so much attention put on each other, it still took a few months for them to get into any kind of argument. And when they did, it was just a tiny fight. Kerry was pretty sure it was her depression. She was drunk, and she tried to get him to break up with her, by showing him just a little bit of how crazy she was. That way, she wouldn't be too attached when he really did break up with her. Kerry was so afraid because it had been just a few weeks, and she was hit hard by all his charms. She hated being away from him, and all she wanted to do was kiss him and be in his arms. So, she started a fight, not 100% purposefully, and yet definitely wanting him to tell her how much he hated her. Kerry was so afraid of getting hurt even worse. So, after a few words between them, nothing Kerry would later regret (she learned not to say anything she would regret when she used to fight with Angelica), just words, which resulted in Kerry grabbing her car keys and running outdoors. It was January, and she didn't even grab a coat, just her keys and cigarettes, the priorities, right? And Candie followed her outside, refusing to let her leave alone. Kerry took her along, as she drove through town, crying harder and harder. Kerry already regretted starting with him, and she was afraid he really would break up with her now. Kerry knew he hated her, and he was just an illusion her mentally unstable mind had cooked up. He was just too good to be true, that's all. Kerry turned a corner and saw his car. Her heart leapt. Was he just going home because he was going to just stop coming over, like Cole had stopped calling? Or was he looking for her? Kerry headed home, nonetheless, her rear-wheel-drive car sliding all over the place, and she heard Matthew's car tires squeal. She prayed he would be okay, he was drunk too, and the last thing he needed was an underage. Kerry was sure his parents would just love her then. Kerry pulled into her parking spot at the apartment, glanced around for cops before she got out (old habits do die hard), and Candie and Kerry headed for the door. Squealing tires stopped Kerry dead in her tracks, and she turned to see Matthew coming back. Actually coming back to her. Would he yell at her, tell her how truly insane she really was, and that he never wanted to see her again? Would he just throw the apartment key out the car window and not say a word? Her heart raced wondering what he'd say. Wondering if there was enough beer to help her feel better after she was alone again. As he parked his car, Kerry asked Candie to wait upstairs so they could talk alone. He came over to her, and she just stood there bawling (the second Candie shut the door the tears had begun), wanting to tell him how sorry she was and how much he meant to her. Yet she stood there in silence, petrified of what he would say. He said he was upset about her freaking out, and he didn't want to break up with her, but he'd been through a girlfriend who had done this all the time and even worse, and if Kerry did it a lot, a relationship wouldn't work out between them. Through her tears and her thick voice, Kerry said she would try to never do it again, and she cried over and over again that she was sorry. The snow came down all around them, and she waited still to hear him tell her it was over, short and sweet, bye-bye, see ya later, adios, amiga. Standing there, it hit Kerry like a punch in the gut, she was in love with him. That was why her chest ached so badly, and why she wanted to kiss him and cry with him, and hold him. She cried harder, and he just looked at her and said, "Kerry, I've wanted to tell you this, because I've felt this way for awhile, but I was afraid to. Kerry, I love you."

Immediately, Kerry's chest fell in, and her heart eased. She cried a little harder, but it wasn't from sadness this time. He loved her; he really said that, right? Waves of reassurance filled her as she barely choked out that she loved him, too. He said she had to stop freaking out, but that he really did love her. She thought, *I'll never get sick of hearing him say that to me.*

He held her close as they kissed under the snowflake-ridden sky, the stars illuminating their faces, and glistening off of Kerry's tears. Kerry suddenly felt quite warm out on the sidewalk, and he dried her tears with fluttering kisses on her cheeks. Kerry suddenly felt that with him by her side, she'd never cry again, and she'd never need to have a little weed party alone, because he would protect her from everything, past and present. They rejoined the party, and that night, they made love. It was the greatest sex ever, because it wasn't just sex, they were making love. Before sleep overtook her, still in his loving arms, she wondered what she had done to find Matthew. She had been afraid she might not want a man ever again after Chase and Cole, but here she was, madly in love with Matthew.

46

They did end up having a little falling out period, but it was because they had been spending every minute of every day with each other. He decided he needed a break from Kerry, and she was again so afraid he was going to break up with her. He stayed away for about two or three days, and Kerry had never felt so alone in those few days than she had in her whole life. He came back the one night and slept there with her, but left the next morning. That week, miserable as it was, really helped their relationship though. They realized that they loved each other very much, but they couldn't smother each other.

Kerry thought immediately after hearing about her most recent pap smear results that he would want to take off running. The doctor told her that it wasn't a sexually transmitted disease, but the cells were definitely not supposed to be there, and they needed to be removed. Kerry was going to have to have them surgically removed, but it wasn't really considered a surgery. Kerry considered it a surgery, but she wasn't going to be knocked out or anything. They numbed the surface of her…area…and proceeded to freeze it for three minutes, then scald it for three minutes, then freeze it for another three minutes, then scald it for the last three minutes. She was horrified that they had lied about how unbelievably painful it was, and since she had to really strain not to cry, she was getting angry about not being warned. They even had the nerve to ask if she was willing to let students watch. Were they kidding? No way! Anyway, she couldn't have sex for a month afterwards, and she truly thought Matthew would get freaked out by the fact that there was something wrong with her in her "woman parts," and he would get scared and leave, whether he loved her or not. But he was more worried that anything, and he stuck with Kerry through it all, every appointment, every painful night's sleep, and every time she had her period, and the PMS was truly worse because of that pain. He stood beside her through everything.

He convinced her she was not crazy, or depressed, so she took herself off the depression medications. No winding down, just cold turkey off of them. She had a few fits in the first few weeks without them, but after her hands stopped shaking from not having them, she was fine. Matthew was her new drug, and she was addicted.

Soon, he started talking about the Army, and his interest in joining. It scared the shit out of Kerry, and depressed her, so she avoided thinking of him even considering it. He forced her to talk about it, since it wasn't just his future, but theirs, and he relieved some of her fears, but there were always those nagging ones that just woudn't leave. Candie's ex-husband went into the Marines, and they were divorced by the time he was assigned to his first base. He had found someone else. At the time, this really shocked Kerry, because he wasn't really the best guy anyway, but Candie was broken-hearted. Kerry was petrified Matthew would find someone else. It wouldn't take them long to realize what a catch he was, and Kerry was so scared of losing him.

Their relationship was great; she tried her best not to go crazy and not to start fights. She did a few times when she had drunk a bit too much, but he stuck with her, and she had to give him credit for that. She thought most of the time, she really was trying to get him to break up with her. She just knew the longer he stayed, the harder she would take it. She had taken so long to recover from all those previous men she had dated, and she loved Matthew, and had never loved any of them. It was so much easier to be depressed and let everyone pay attention to you, and to take pills than it was to be happy. To actually try to make a relationship into a loving one. This one was going to hurt, and Kerry knew it was inevitable. And she just wasn't sure she was going to be able to recover.

47

Kerry and Matthew ended up having this party at the apartment one night, and it turned out half of their little town showed up. Really, almost fifty people crammed into her little two-bedroom apartment. It turned out that a party in the woods had almost been busted, someone had called Matthew, and they all came to her place. Kerry didn't care, because Candie wasn't home and she was lonely. Soon, though, Kerry's landlady came upstairs (she had a business downstairs that she had been late leaving, doing some paperwork). She stuck her head in the door and started screaming for Kerry or Candie. Kerry was sitting on the floor, legs crossed, and singing, when somebody told her to look at the front door. Kerry was totally out of it, toasted as all hell, just staring at the woman as she screamed that Kerry had two weeks to get the hell out, and then Kerry laughed and said , "Get out of my house, bitch!" Kerry was still laughing when she slammed the door and turned around to go back to sitting on the floor. She just didn't care. A few minutes later her cell phone rang, and one of her buddies that actually worked for the landlady warned her that somebody (wonder who) had clued the police in, and the house was vacant in about two minutes. Kerry was shocked; if she had only known it was that easy to vacate a house! The remaining partiers (Matthew, Belle, Owen, and Kerry) hid all the beer, moved what was in the fridge to the closet (to hide it; nobody that was left was 21), and they tried to put stuff on top of the beer in the garbage. They all brushed their teeth, rinsed, and turned out all the lights. Not too long after, somebody was rapping at the door. Belle, her boyfriend, Owen, and Kerry had run into the bedroom to change into pajamas, and Matthew was in the bathroom.

Kerry tried to pretend everyone was sleeping and nobody moved. Then the police threatened to knock the door down (and Kerry wasn't sure if they were allowed to do that or not, but she wasn't about to pay for a door when she just got evicted) so she rubbed her eyes and answered, still pretending she had been sleeping. The two officers just paraded in without asking and started walking around, looking for everyone. The female cop walked in on Matthew while he was in the bathroom! That was the funniest thing. He was trying to finish brushing his teeth, and she asked him to get dressed (he was just wearing shorts) and come out. They put the four of them in the living room while they checked the apartment, asked about the beer in the garbage (our over 21 friends had left earlier), and lectured us. Nothing happened though, other than that eviction. It worried Kerry to have to explain to Candie why they'd have to move, but other than that, her buzz kept her happy. The eviction didn't bother her at all; she had just quit her job at the mall, because her boss was putting too much stress on her anyway, and since she could no longer afford rent, she now had a solid excuse to go home to Angelica. Worked out for Kerry for the best actually. She called Candie, who wanted to take Matthew and Kerry out to go look for a new place. The next week they looked around, but nothing popped out, and Kerry still hadn't found a job, so she took Matthew and moved in with her mom. Kerry practically took or went with him anywhere, so he pretty much lived with her anyway.

In reference to the mall job, Kerry was so wound up in Matthew, that it actually depressed her out to go to work, but she went, and worked her ass off in order to make the day go faster. After her previous promotion to sales supervisor, she had more responsibilities (and the money to be able to move in with Candie). Kerry was awesome, and that extra workload made her feel like she was accomplishing something every day. Her grandmother had gotten sick a few times recently though, and she had switched her shift a few times in order to be with her at the hospital, and it turned out her boss hated that. Her boss wanted Kerry's job to be her top priority, and Kerry couldn't do that. She put so much misery on Kerry for having such good initiative, that Kerry ended up waiting until she was at lunch one day, putting her shirt and keys on the desk in her boss' office, and just walking out. It scared the shit out of Kerry even then, because she had never been the type of person to just walk out on anything. Even those horrible relationships that she didn't like, and that only made her miserable, she felt like she had to work on them. She felt that it was her fault they didn't work out. But she couldn't handle anything her boss was dishing out on her, so she just left. She knew she had to find another job soon though. Bills didn't care about personal problems, and after all the running around with Mary and all the advances for the weed, she had racked up quite a bit of credit card debt.

The results of the procedure Kerry had recently had, the one where they removed the "bad cells," came back that the cells that showed up were pre-cancerous. The doctors and the nurse explained to her that what that meant was that there wasn't a certainty that they would become cancerous, but that they needed to be removed in order to prevent the possibility of cancer. Since Kerry had already had the first "surgery," they checked her for a routine follow-up and saw the cells had returned. The second procedure they would be trying would be while Matthew was planning on being in boot camp, so the "no sex for a month afterwards" didn't bother Kerry this time. It did bother her that there were abnormal cells growing possibly cancerously where they shouldn't be…or even at ALL, but she was doing everything she could in order to remove them, and she wouldn't have Matthew there to tempt her to want to have sex. The procedure was more painful than they prepared her for (AGAIN), and she was biting her lip in order not to let the tears prickling her eyes escape. She didn't want to appear as a frail little girl. But then they told her that they couldn't believe how well she had held up. She should have known they were going to lie about this procedure, too.

48

Towards Kerry's birthday in April, Matthew's Army thoughts got even more serious, and he was going to visit the recruiter more often. Kerry dreaded each visit, because that had to be it for them. Kerry told Matthew she was willing to wait, but he didn't want her to. He also started acting strangely and, Kerry thought to herself, selfishly. He would go to parties without her, never cheating on her (to her knowledge), but just the not-inviting her part hurt her feelings, and reminded her of her depression. He just started acting differently. Kerry clung to him though, because after all she had done to try to get him to break up with her, she wasn't giving up now that she knew what she wanted.

He went to his meeting for the Army May 31, and he called Kerry and said he wouldn't be home when he thought he would be. Kerry told him she could pick him up whenever he was ready, but he said, "No, I'm leaving for Benning today; I won't see you for fourteen weeks or more."

Kerry bit her tongue and told him she loved him, and he said it too, and he said he had the address and the phone numbers, and he would get in touch with her as soon as possible. The whole world caved in when she hung up that phone. She felt so alone, and so lost, already! She was used to spending twenty-four hours a day with him, seven days a week, and now she was going to have nothing, nothing at all, for five months. He went infantry, *all the way, baby*, and then he was going to jump school, for his Airborne wings. Kerry was so lost. She went and picked her Aunt Janine up, crying, and she hugged Kerry like she was her own daughter, and held her until the tears slowed down. Kerry just felt so alone, and that is what she loved about Matthew so much, that alone feeling that just disappeared the second he looked at her. Kerry never had to feel like she wasn't worth anything, because he was always there for her. Now she had to depend on herself once again, and that hadn't worked for years, so she felt so screwed. She almost wanted to call her doctor to get refills on the depression medication she had gone so long without. The only thing she had was Trooper, the Beagle puppy he had given her a few weeks earlier. It would be the most spoiled puppy ever. Letters and phone calls, they were going to be nothing compared to what Kerry had just lost. The Army had stolen it. Kerry felt very patriotic though, for the first time since 9/11, and she was proud her baby would be fighting for their country.

Kerry got a phone call a few days after, but she wasn't home, she just saw it on the caller ID. She was so depressed that day, so she called up a friend and they got drunk. She saw it as a bad omen that she had missed the first phone call. But he did call the next day, and she got to talk to him for a bit. The sooner he got out of mid-range, which is just sort of a stop on the way to boot camp, the better, because he couldn't graduate until he started!

49

The first thing she got was a postcard, Airborne proudly displayed on the front, and it showed paratroopers landing and headed toward their, well, she could only assume battle, but let's pretend they were heading to a party. With all the craziness overseas, Kerry was well aware her baby was going to end up going over there, and she tried her best not to think of war, and not to watch the news. Anyway, back to her postcard, her heart leapt, the first piece of mail!

> *Hey, baby,*
> *I love, miss, and cherish you but I'm doing fine. I hope you got my message. I'm in midrange now, hope I'll ship soon to basic to get it over with. I'm getting closer with some of the guys, but I still miss you, guys, so tell both moms and my dad I'll write soon. Bye, baby.*

The next letter stated he would start basic June 7, so that Kerry could start marking her calendar. He would start out his letters Dearest, Baby, Love, Carebear, and he wrote sweet words, making her light-headed, her head pound, and her heart ache from him not being here. It wasn't easy, but every day the mail came and there was a letter, relief flooded over her. His mother and her were on a weekly update. If she got mail she called Kerry, and if Kerry got mail she called his mom. Kerry was getting much closer to his family, and they made her feel great. She had been accepted. And his father was like the model of the father she had always wanted. And it didn't bother him when Kerry called him Daddy. At last, someone worthy of that title, that didn't already have a title, like uncle. Somebody that didn't have to feel responsible for someone else's mistake. Matthew kept Kerry's heart light, though, and she made sure to tell him she wasn't hiding away in the house waiting for him. She kept herself as busy as possible while she was waiting for him.

> *Give all the family love for me, if you haven't found another to replace me, which would hurt, but I'd understand.*

> *God, I miss you. I didn't realize how much I loved you, until you weren't around all the time. Let's see how it goes though. I still don't expect you to wait for me, but it is your choice. I still can't promise you anything. I love you, but if it's too hard for you, move on, baby.*

He seemed so scared he'd return to find that Kerry had given up on them. He didn't know her determination. He was everything Kerry had never had, everything she had always wanted in a lover, and in a soul-mate. She would never give up. She would never leave him, being away from him made her want him even more. He had warned her in a talk they had before he left, that he was definitely not ready for marriage, but he loved her, and he hoped they made it to that day when he would be ready for that next step. Kerry stayed dedicated, she never (well, tried *really hard* on this) thought of the future. Kerry wasn't worried about marrying him, she just wanted to stay in love with him. To stay in the moment with him. She wrote to him every single day. Even if she didn't have anything to say, she'd write how much she loved him, and how much she missed him. She just wanted him to have as much mail as possible. He deserved it. This was the hardest thing Kerry had ever had to do though; she would hang out with her friends, but since she had secluded herself with Matthew, it wasn't the same, and she was sad most of the time.

June

The first weekend alone, Kerry went to a weekend camp with his mother, sister, and Belle. Kerry tried to forget all about him being away, and tried to feel as if it was a vacation. She took Belle in case there was weirdness in the family and Kerry felt out of place, but that didn't happen; on the contrary, Belle was suddenly part of the family, too. The vacation didn't work for Kerry, but she did have a good time, and they took lots of pictures to send to Matthew. Kerry ended up getting sick towards the end of the trip though, bad stomach pains and chest pains. She took some pain pills and figured she'd go to the doctor when they got back.

> *Remember when I told you I wouldn't mention parting, well there is one thing I have to tell you. It's nothing like that, I promise. But if you find someone else back home, please wait 'til you see me to tell me. I have been thinking about it for about a week. I heard about some dude that got a "Dear John" letter. And he was okay with it. I wouldn't be. I would wanna die, especially in the environment I'm in now. So, baby, please don't tell me. I'm getting choked up just talking about it now.*

Kerry didn't anticipate finding anyone, but what if when they saw each other on graduation day, it wasn't the same? What if the spark was missing, and Kerry was putting a higher image of Matthew in her head than was actually there? What if he was doing the same thing? Kerry had lost weight just before she met him, and was down to where she felt sexy most of the time, but what if she gained some weight? What if she wasn't as sexy as she thought, and he remembered something different and was disappointed when he came back? Kerry drove herself insane with these thoughts daily. But his letters had absolutely no inclination that he thought of her as anything but the sexiest woman alive. He did that. Kerry thought of that every day. Not once before she had met Matthew had she found herself sexy. He gave her that confidence.

> *Hey, babe, I got an idea, every day at 4:00, look at the sky. I'll do the same; for an instant we'll see each other, not only in our dreams anymore.*

Kerry cried at almost every letter. How could some girl send a Dear John letter? That poor boy left and was hoping to come home to his love again, and she sent him a letter, after not even a month!? It was unreal. She could never do that anyway. It was around this time he first mentioned his hip starting to bother him. That made her worry, because it hadn't even been a month; was this a bad sign?

> *I love you to death, but I miss you even more. I had that picture of you and my sister at camp drinking in my helmet during the road march today. I think I'm gonna do that more often.*

July

Kerry's stomach pains didn't get better, and they sent her to the hospital for an ultra-sound of her stomach. No, there was no pregnancy, they just don't know what is causing the pain. She would get the results shortly, but damn, that pain was unbelievable.

His letters came pretty regularly, and he sent money so they could pay off some bills. Some were just Kerry's bills, but also stuff he had bought on her credit cards. He also sent her a dog-tag necklace with *"I belong to a soldier"* engraved on it, and a shot glass from his base. She had applied at a few jobs, to help with the bills too, but she only worked at each a short time, because she just couldn't concentrate. That and she had to have her phone on 24/7, because there was no way she was missing a phone call from Georgia. He didn't get to call often, and there was no way a part-time minimum-wage job was holding her from him. He ran through her head day in and day out, and he was all she could think of. She worried constantly, about his hip and his ankle, which he had sprained on the one road march, and she just wanted him to succeed so badly, because he deserved it. He worked so hard to get where he was, and she wasn't sure he knew how great he really was. Kerry started checking stuff out online, hotel prices and such, because she knew she was staying as long as she could with him when he graduated. And he should have a weekend free before he started jump school, which lasts three weeks, and it's not as strict. He could have visitors and stay off base if he pleased. Which meant more phone calls and that made Kerry happier!

50

    This month was Kerry's Uncle Danny's wedding reception, as he had taken his bride to Bermuda to get married. They had been together forever, but her Uncle Danny finally made her Aunt Andrea officially Kerry's aunt. Kerry was so thrilled about this, because he was the only root she considered family on *that* side of her life. She had gotten a lot closer to him as well, and he was another father figure in her life. He approved of Matthew, and that made her heart sing; he had actually called Cameron a fag the one time Kerry took him over there. And horribly enough she had to bite her tongue not to laugh. Kerry didn't mean anything by it, but she had wanted to make her "relationship" with Cameron more physical and he had said no, so what kind of man was he anyway? But Uncle Danny made her feel Matthew was real, and his letters that streamed in made her feel so loved. Really and truly loved.

> *I just got done talking to you on the phone. I feel luckier every day. But the hardest is yet to come. But don't worry.*

    Kerry's daily worries hadn't eased as time went on, and now that he had been gone awhile, no, she wasn't used to not having him around, but it was a tiny bit easier getting his letters weekly, but her worry was, what if he was in love with her, and then when they saw each other the flame had died out? Kerry didn't want that to be true no matter what, but there's always the what-if, and she was the queen of thinking them up. She hated the what-if's because they drove her insane. She couldn't get them out of her head. He had mentioned marriage in the last letter, and he said he wasn't ready for it, but he felt a next step coming on. That confused her, and she refused to get her hopes up. She couldn't bear to expect a ring and then not get one.

You're too good for me, baby.

The doctor decided she had gallstones, and she would need her gallbladder out. This upset Kerry, because what if (see there's another what if) she had to go into surgery around the time he graduated? She could never miss his graduation! She tried to schedule the appointment as early as possible, because they said she'd need four weeks recovery time, and she figured she could make it that way. But they couldn't schedule it yet anyway. More tests and appointments first.

Okay, Mrs. Kilchern, yes, I said it, nice ring to it, huh? Remember, time will tell, but it does sound nice. I love you, Kerry Kilchern.

I love you
Always & Forever
Near & Far
We'll stick together
Everywhere I will be with you
Everything I will do for you.

After he begged a little bit, Kerry did end up sending him provocative pictures, and he rather enjoyed them. So at least he was happy in his far-away temporary home. Besides, he only had about seven weeks left, and after he had made it this far, he deserved a few pictures of what he was missing by being away. It was really embarrassing to have Belle take photos of her naked, and in most of them, Kerry was trying not to laugh.

I failed my PT test, and the drill sergeant was thinking of restarting me, but I can't let that happen. I already miss you too much, and knowing there is only seven weeks left, I need to do it. I love you so much, baby. I need a lot of support right now, give it all you got. I really don't know what to say other than I'm sorry.

Kerry thought what bothered her the most was not being able to be with him, and to take care of him. That gave her purpose when he was around, getting him things, taking care of everything she could for him, and now she was helpless. She wanted to hold him and tell him he could do the PT test, it was all in his mind, and he just could. She knew it.

He got a scare when the mail was messed up and he wasn't getting the regular pile of mail, but she reassured him, and sent a few extra just in case. Kerry didn't know what happened, but she supposed the post office has that happen sometimes.

He had a lot of training, in and out of the field, so the letters got a little farther between, but each time he reassured her it was because of training, and he would love to write to her and talk to her every day. Kerry was counting down the days, and she was so excited to see him.

51

August

The beginning of August led Kerry to go on another camping trip with Matthew's sister, her husband, Jake, and a few friends. It was a well-deserved vacation, and Kerry had the best time with his sister Mel, and his cousin Mindy, and Belle. The five of them were nothing but troublemakers the whole weekend, and it was the best time. Kerry got to relax, was still able to get drunk nightly, and not worry about Matthew as much, because their schedule kept them pretty busy. They toured the campgrounds, got drunk, swam in the river near the tents, and relaxed in the shade of the trees. Kerry came home with a hot tan, and she was totally exhausted. But it was well worth it. And it made Kerry feel like she was actually part of the family. Mel assured her that no matter what happened between her and Matthew, that Kerry would always be welcome in Mel's home, and she already considered Kerry a sister. It was great to have someone say that to her, especially since the two ingrates that her biological father had given her had only shunned Kerry for her entire life.

The next letter Kerry received told her that there was an overnight pass. Kerry would have to drive the fourteen hours to Georgia, and they would only have one night together, but that seemed totally worth it to her!

Kerry had her buddy Owen go with her, and she drove the fourteen hours down to Georgia, leaving in the afternoon, so that if she drove all night, they'd be there by the time he got his pass at noon. Kerry's heart was racing the whole drive! She had her camera, and she was excited! (And horny!) Kerry just couldn't believe she would get to see him; she was so scared that they'd get halfway and he would call and say the pass was revoked. She had the hotel reservation, Owen had gotten his own room, and they were ready! Kerry took a three-hour nap around 4 A.M., and Owen said he couldn't sleep because Kerry had parked behind some big rigs, and he was on bodyguard duty. Whatever, Kerry was exhausted; she didn't care if he sat up and shot spitballs at the trucks, she needed a nap so she didn't sleep the whole time she got to see Matthew! When they finally got there, he called her cell, and she told him where her and Owen were (that base was very confusing and they were at the wrong spot for an hour), but they finally parked in the right area, and that's when he called to ask where they were. When Kerry told him, and he said, "No, shit!" and hung up. Um...she was surprised, but got out, because she had to assume he knew where they were and he was close, and she ended up being right; he came running up the hill at lightning speed, and he picked Kerry up and swung her around, and kissed her, and held her like he hadn't thought he'd ever see her again! It was like a shot out of a romantic movie, and Kerry had never had that happen in her entire life. She hadn't even though it possible to happen to her. She almost cried, holding onto him so tightly, and when he put her down, she stood right beside him, for fear he would disappear. He had lost a lot of weight, put on a lot of muscle, and God was he sexy! Kerry decided that uniform had to come off! Kerry let him drive, and he showed Owen and her around the base, explaining what this and that was for, and what he had done there. It was all fascinating, but the best part was that he was in the car with her, holding her hand, and every time he looked at her, she had to have blushed. Now she knew why it was worth waiting for. After you haven't seen the love of your life, you realize how much they mean to you, how much you love them. How could anyone ever let that go?

LIVING AS A MISTAKE

They spent the best night together, took a hot bubble bath, and he was so romantic and attentive, and it was just the absolute best sex ever. Kerry slept so peacefully in his arms, because that was what she had been missing the most. The best part of a relationship is falling asleep feeling you are so protected, and there's absolutely no vulnerability. He had to be dropped off at eleven the next morning, and Kerry already dreaded the drive back home. Actually she wanted to camp out on base until he graduated and then she could take him home with her. She still couldn't believe it was August. Kerry hadn't seen him since May, and he was the most gorgeous thing she had ever laid eyes on. Soon he would graduate, hopefully in about four weeks. Then she'd get to see him, and in uniform again! That was the best part of the Army, that uniform just made the sexiest man even *more* desirable. They made sure to take pictures for their parents, and then they parted. Kerry didn't want him to let her go, but they got into the car, and she dropped him off at his barracks. At least she got to kiss him good-bye this time. She kept thinking, remembering the measly phone call telling her he was leaving the first time. And it was almost over. That part scared her as well as excited her. There were no girls, no clubs, and no fun during basic. But after this, he had three weeks of jump school, and he was allowed to go out at night. Then his month of "vacation" at home, then he was stationed in North Carolina. Complete freedom there. Without Kerry. She'll be left alone to wonder what he's doing yet again.

52

We did Eagle Run, but I about passed out; it was like 98 degrees outside. I think I drank enough water because I wasn't feeling well all day so I think it was just the heat. I'm okay though, baby, it was you that kept me running. Your beautiful face, smile, and texture. I knew if I stopped I might not be seeing you for awhile. I couldn't deal with that. I love you dearly, baby.

The doctor decided Kerry needed her gallbladder out finally, so great! Not really, that depressed her, she'd never had major surgery, or minor for that matter, and now she'd have to do it while he's away. He graduated September 13, so Kerry worked on scheduling her appointment for September 2, hoping she would feel better for the drive. But it had to come out, and Angelica said she'd drive with Kerry for the graduation. So at least she'd have help for the drive.

Kerry sent letters warning him of her surgery, because she wouldn't be able to write while in the hospital. But she prepared the night before, and her mother drove her in. Clean and sterile, she got her IVs and was wheeled into the operating room. There they gave her something to put her to sleep and told her to count backwards from one hundred. Kerry was amused to think that she got one hundred out, when she woke up. Her stomach hurt, and her throat was sore from the tube they put into it, but she felt okay. Until the pain medication wore off. They told her she'd have to spend the night in the hospital, and that pissed her off. She would much rather be at home and be miserable, but they said no. Angelica stayed with her all night, and she had a few visitors, but when it came time to rest, the nurses gave her green Jell-O and some pills. They did not mix, and soon Kerry had green bed sheets as well. The nurse came and changed them, and Kerry had to have help to get up every time she had to use the bathroom, because to bend over was to inflict stabbing pains into her abdomen. Then her mother tried to help her adjust the bed, but she had to do it herself, and she broke the bed. The bottom rose up and instead of stopping, it started jumping at the top! The pain seared through Kerry's stomach and all over her chest, and instead of pushing the nurse button, Kerry felt it would be a much better idea to just scream for her. Which worked better than she had imagined. She came in, did something to the bed, gave Kerry some more medicine that almost knocked her out, and sent for a new bed. Therefore, when Kerry and Angelica left the next day, the nurses said good-bye gratefully. Kerry was wheeled outside and helped into the car, with bottles of happiness in her possession. When she got home, she slept, woke up, took a pill, and went back to sleep. That was the routine for the next week, taking a few minutes of time awake to write to Matthew and let him know she was okay.

53

It was getting close, and from his letters he was obviously excited that it was almost over.

> Dear Kerry,
> I know I just wrote you but it never seems to be enough. I've endured a lot being stuck down here. I know you and this relationship have as well. Kerry, you're so beautiful, and guys are probably too intimidated by your beauty to ask you out, others may have asked you out and you turned them down because you "think" I'm the greatest. You are. You have been the backbone of this relationship. I love you, baby, and no matter what happens in the future I always will. You have been the best thing that's ever happened to me. For you, no matter how hard it gets, no matter how bad I want to fall out of training, I'll see your face and hear your voice and drive on. I never wanna fail you, embarrass you, trap you, and most of all hurt you. You hold the loving part of my heart as I train the other part to accept any death I may come across in the future. I'm a trained lover by you and killer by Army. I prefer the love. We'll be together soon, baby. Never have I loved someone so much. It's important that you remember that no matter what.

LIVING AS A MISTAKE

September 13

It was time; finally, everyone was headed to Georgia to see Matthew graduate! His mom and dad were flying and staying at a nearby hotel, and Kerry and Angelica had the same hotel room where Matthew and Kerry had stayed for their little night of romance. The first ceremony was the Turning Blue ceremony, where his dad got to adorn him with his blue cord, for infantry. It was all very professional, and very interesting. Kerry had lost some more weight with her stress-worn summer without Matthew, and she was wearing a tiny blue dress. Matthew kept sneaking glances at her, and she could feel her heart pound in her head; she felt it would deafen the audience. The guys all looked so grown-up, even though some of them had to have recently graduated high school. But Kerry's baby, he looked so sexy, and so important. She wasn't even sure how to describe how it felt to see him in uniform, and to know that he was now somebody to respect and to give recognition to. She personally knew he didn't think that way, he was doing something he had wanted to do for a long time, but he really did deserve everything anybody could give him. He got to a weight he felt sexy at, and he had accomplished something big. He was a soldier. An infantry soldier.

The graduation ceremony was very interesting; they opened with tanks and demonstrations with camouflaged men in suits that looked like bushes, and then the men marched out. There was more than one class graduating, so it took awhile, but their group just concentrated on trying to pinpoint Matthew's location. They did speeches and awards and marched the men back out. As they marched out, the entire family took pictures of him, and then they got to take pictures of him on the graduation area, with the infantry flags in the background. To Matthew, this wasn't an accomplishment for him; he had just wanted to make his father proud of him. Kerry always found that odd, because his father always acted so proud of him, but it was as if Matthew couldn't see it. He was always trying to outdo something or somebody to make his father proud. They got to meet Matthew later, after pictures and everything, and the whole group went out to dinner. Kerry's stomach wasn't very well from the surgery, so she ate very little, but it didn't matter, she was living high on life lately, which was a good thing, because she hadn't touched any weed since their weekend together. She was so happy to be around Matthew every day, that it didn't matter what happened anywhere else, and so far, she hadn't had a hard time giving up the weed and the pills. She was still drinking, but not blacking out, and this was small of her, but she still felt that it was an accomplishment. The fact that she was with him, taking bubble baths every night, watching a movie in his arms, having that totally indescribable sex yet again, it was just like a dream.

They explored the base with their family, and the town, and had a wonderful time with his parents and Kerry's mom. His parents had to leave earlier than Kerry and Angelica, though, and they saw them off to their flight after a few days. Kerry and her mother stayed until he started jump school.

Mark, Kerry's "friend from the beginning," was getting married in a few weeks, so Kerry couldn't stay the entire time with Matthew (not that Angelica could have taken that much time off work anyway). But they stayed and Kerry enjoyed herself immensely; it was so great to fall asleep with him every night, and to talk and drink, and just be with him. After the time apart, Kerry felt she could live without him, but never wanted to again, and she definitely didn't want to leave him again. They talked about Kerry staying there while he was in jump school. After Mark's wedding, having Kerry drive back down there, and staying until he graduated, and then they would drive to North Carolina together. The idea appealed to Kerry; it meant only half the time apart from each other! The hotel they had chosen was cheap enough that it was an affordable cost, and since Kerry had to go to the wedding (she was the female best man), then she wouldn't be staying the whole three weeks anyway. Parting time was difficult again though, and Kerry dreaded it as well as hating its arrival. But she was getting sick more often, and her stomach was aching, so she was grateful for the fourteen-hour nap she got. Angelica ended up driving the entire way home. Kerry dreamed of Matthew the whole time.

54

When Angelica and Kerry got to North Carolina, they immediately had to prepare and drive to Pennsylvania for Mark's wedding. Kerry was an oddball as the best man considering she was female, but Mark and his new bride, Justina, really made it elegant, because they helped Kerry choose an outfit that was tuxedo-ish, but still very feminine, and the pictures turned out excellent, and Kerry was truly excited to finally truly love her body and feel like flaunting it. Kerry really enjoyed herself there, even though the one gentleman in the wedding kept flirting with her, and it was nice, but it made her want Matthew there more. She spoke with Matthew on the phone one night after the wedding, and they fought for the most part of the conversation, debating on their own future, but it turned out fine, and just kept Kerry from having a good night's sleep. Him and a few of the guys in his class had gotten a hotel room and partied, and he had called Kerry after he was already drunk. Kerry wasn't sure what he wanted to do, but he didn't seem to want to break up with her, just to explain that he still wasn't ready for marriage. Maybe because of Mark's wedding, he thought she had implied something, but if she had, she certainly didn't mean to. She wasn't ready for marriage yet either. She was just worried he was going to find someone else, now that he had his freedom back, and he was so far away from her. Mark's wedding did make some gears start turning in her head, and she was jealous, she admitted freely to Mark. But she also admitted she was pretty sure every girl has that jealous twinge when it is another girl's Big Day. Even as great a girl Justina was, Kerry was still jealous because it was that "best day" type of thing. At the reception, the little girl who caught the bouquet actually gave it to Kerry and said, "Here; you'll need this before me." That made Kerry nervous, and made Mark and Justina burst out into waves of laughter. But Kerry was still very happy for Mark. After all these years and everything he had been through, he deserved to be happy. Now he had his family, because Justina already had a baby whose father was nowhere to be found. Kerry was sad they were so very far from home, though. She knew when their group left, she wasn't going to get to see Mark, Justina, or their baby for a very long time. On the other hand, when they got back to North Carolina, Kerry got to drive down and see *her* baby again. She realized she had made her life revolve around Matthew. And she loved it.

The drive down was a lot rougher on Kerry this, hopefully, last time. It was painful, that damn surgery hadn't really helped her pain yet, just gave her new pain, and she was alone this time, so it was a little scarier. She kept her thoughts on the road, and sang the whole way down there. It was getting easier to drive the distance; after all, this was how many trips to Georgia, and now she had also been to Pennsylvania, so she was really just driving up and down the east coast. One of Matthew's buddies had a girlfriend who was also staying at the hotel, so at least Kerry did have someone to talk to. They chatted about what their future plans were, and this girl had a "promise" ring and was surprised that Kerry did not wear a ring. She even tried to talk Matthew into buying Kerry a promise ring, but Kerry was so happy he said it was a stupid idea. If he decided Kerry was what he wanted, Kerry did want a promise, but she wanted it to be a proposal, a real one, not JUST a promise. And if he needed time, time was what Kerry was willing to give him.

This graduation was very neat, too. Kerry went with her new friend, and she got to pin his Airborne wings on Matthew. Kerry felt too proud that she was there to cheer him on for his latest accomplishment. It wasn't everyone that made it through jump school. Kerry felt her baby was doing so much, and she couldn't wait to let him know enough how proud she was of him. And now she got to take him home! She was just a little disappointed that her treasured nights at their hotel were going to become memories, but he was coming home with her, and they were going to make new memories. His 21st birthday was coming up, and they had to go home and celebrate! Her only worry and jealousy there, was that she wasn't going to be 21 for another six months. He was going to be able to go to the bar and dance and flirt, and Kerry would have to stay at home. Alone. Almost all her friends were 21, and she was the baby. Dammit.

55

Home. Finally, Matthew was at home. They visited family together, he went and visited his friends, and Kerry just reveled in the joy that he was home. He did come back a bit different, though, and it seemed like he wanted to explore all options of town, without Kerry there all the time like before. But he did spend a lot of time with her, just not *all* his time. There were a few times that he wanted to spend time with friends that Kerry was specifically not invited, and that hurt. It made her wonder why she couldn't go. What was he doing? One was a girl he said used to be in love with him, and it would make her uncomfortable to have Kerry there. Kerry hated that. If he was in love with her, as he said he was, it shouldn't matter who they visited. And if this girl just wanted him to be happy, she should be happy that he found someone to love. It made her feel like her old self, just there for convenience. In a way Kerry hated Matthew for making her feel that way, but at the same time, he had just done so much, and he deserved to see all his friends. It made her so afraid that he had realized that he wanted to see the world alone first though. That was how he acted, up until the day he was to leave. That good-bye kiss felt like a real good-bye, and it scared Kerry almost to death. She tried her best not to cry, but it felt like he was going away, and not coming back. Not going to call, just going to leave. Thanks for the support before, it was great, but I don't need you now. It petrified her to think that way, but he was never in his life in the shape he was in now, or so he told Kerry so many times, and he wanted to flaunt it. He told her that he had never had girls stare at him and flirt with him, as he had recently, and he wanted to take advantage of it. He was never unfaithful, he told Kerry every time a girl was brought up, and she believed him…for the most part. She couldn't blame him, she had been fat her entire life, and now she wasn't either, and she had that too; guys she graduated with giving her looks, and staring at her, while they had called her names and laughed at her for all those years before. She knew how good it felt; how could she deny him that? But at the same time, what about her? She had denied all men who had flirted with her, who had asked her out, and who had hinted they liked her while he was gone. She loved Matthew, though, and before he left, before he lost any weight, and she didn't care about the weight. She had never deemed it an issue. And, yes, he did look very sexy, and very fit, and the sex was great, because he *felt* sexy and fit, but it wasn't the same. Kerry loved him for who he was, and the looks didn't matter to her. Kerry knew one night, he was going to come back to her, from the bar where she wasn't allowed to go to, and he was going to say to her, some gorgeous girl swept him off his feet, and it would be because of his looks. It wasn't fair, because he had so much more than that, and looks aren't everything. On his 21st birthday, Kerry dropped him off at the bar, and he came home trashed, but it was his birthday, so it was okay. Kerry had driven him so he could get that way, and she picked him up so she could make sure he was safe. He told her he danced and had a great time. And that a sexy girl had kissed him. Kerry's heart fell in then. This was the beginning. It was all going to go downhill. He said it meant nothing, just felt nice to have her want him; he said he didn't want her, and that he had come home to Kerry. He wanted her, not that girl. The words meant nothing after his actions and Kerry's heart had already nearly exploded in her chest. He reassured her that it was nothing, he had come home to her, because he wanted her, Kerry, loved her, Kerry, but he had *kissed* a stranger. Who, it didn't matter, because in a few days, he'd be in North Carolina, with many bars and many beautiful girls who love soldiers. After a long, loud argument about this, they made up, because he was right, he did come home to her, not left with some stranger because she was pretty and obviously fairly easy. But it still hurt so badly. Like it was just the beginning of him starting to lose interest in Kerry. How could she be mad though? Hadn't she wanted someone every time she got a little tipsy and been at a party where some guy, who meant nothing, had tipped her off that he wanted her? Although, to be fair to Kerry, she had never even allowed them to get near kissing her. They talked it out, and they were still *in love*, but Kerry was still scared, maybe not just scared, but petrified. She was so scared of losing him. He was everything to her. Everything.

56

Then, he was gone. A kiss good-bye, and Kerry watched him drive down the driveway, heading onto a new adventure without Kerry by his side. Kentucky was new, exciting, with lots of new drinking buddies, who were, on the most part, single, horny soldiers who would want to head to the bars. Looking for nothing but a good time, and a one-night stand. Kerry felt he was lost to her. He called when he got there, and a few days a week at first. But it was November, and Kerry wouldn't see him again for, well, she didn't know how long. She had just started another school, and she couldn't afford to drive down to visit him whenever she deemed necessary (which was nearly every day she wanted to see him), and he didn't get to drive off base for whatever distance he saw fit. They had limitations on their new soldiers, and he wasn't allowed more than a few hours away, yet Kerry was almost ten hours away. It was a few weeks later when he called and didn't sound right, didn't sound like himself. Kerry had been shopping with Angelica and Belle, but when her cell rang, she went outside the store and sat in the car to talk to him. He told her then what she had expected, yet dreaded hearing for almost a year now: he wanted to see other people. He reassured her they weren't breaking up, but Kerry cried, long and hard. The tears weren't easy for him to hear, and he kept asking her to stop, kept telling her how much he loved her, but if they were going to take the next step, then he decided they needed to see other people to make sure marriage was right for them. When he got married, he wanted to do it only once, and to do it right. Kerry agreed because she felt the same way about marriage, but she didn't want to see other people. She knew what she wanted, and she knew at that moment she was losing it, possibly forever. He was going to find someone prettier, skinnier, and he was going to leave Kerry behind in the dust. They talked for almost an hour, deciding the future of their relationship, which had, up until now, lasted through some very hard times. He said Kerry could call his new cell anytime; he had made them assign it a local number, so that she could call and it would not be long-distance. But it was true, he was going to go out on dates, hug, kiss, and who knows what with someone new. To compare, to make sure Kerry was right for him. Kerry knew she wasn't, she had always known that, and she knew he'd find his true love quickly. They had many clubs and bars, since it was an Army base; they had lots of young, single soldiers, and there were girls aplenty. Kerry was suddenly old news, and she knew it.

The next few weeks were horrible for Kerry; her friends tried setting her up with people, and she would make excuses not to go, and avoiding them became the norm for her. She hated the bad things they said about Matthew, and the fact that they were so quick with finding someone for her to date. Avoiding them made it so she wouldn't have to hear them say how great this hot guy was, and how cute and smart this other guy was. None of them were Matthew, and Kerry was lost. Every time they showed her a picture, or described this new guy to her, she pictured Matthew, and she knew if they showed up and were not what she had imagined, she would be disappointed and would not have fun.

The one night Kerry had talked to Matthew on his cell, and he said he was getting ready to go out to a club, and it was then Kerry knew she needed to get drunk. Fast and hard. She called up some friends, and those friends called up some guys. Kerry smoked after finally finding her old dealer, and she did shots with all these new strangers. She didn't know why they had called these guys up, but they had been trying to set her up for awhile, so she figured she had it coming for avoiding them. They did have a decent time. And for spite, and just to try Matthew's new idea, Kerry flirted with a guy named Timmy. He touched her leg, rubbed her back, and kept telling her how pretty she was. Every time he did, Kerry just smiled at him and took a long drag of a beer or lit up a cigarette. She wasn't sure how cool these guys were, so her pot was hidden in the bathroom for when she needed a big hit. She was getting drunk, was already high, and it felt good. It felt like old times, although she wasn't having her visions and her nightmares of Calvin's hands, so she supposed that was a good sign. Timmy was giving her attention, and that felt good. But the whole thing felt so very wrong to her. Kerry was still wearing her *"I belong to a soldier"* necklace, and Timmy took it off, telling her she was a free woman, free to make her own choices. She had volunteered some of the information about her current situation with him, hoping to get him to understand he didn't really have a chance until she was 100% sure Matthew wasn't coming home to her. She had that thin thread of hope, and she was holding on tightly. Timmy kissed her then, and it was long and deep. Kerry zoned out completely of her mind, kissed him back, and it was nice. But not the same, and not dreamy at all. Kerry knew she'd do that, compare him to Matthew. Which he was not, by a long shot. He was nothing of the man Kerry still loved, and he could never be. But she continued to kiss him, because she wanted to do what Matthew wanted, and every time she pictured in her head Matthew dancing with another girl, his hands on her back, or lower, she grabbed Timmy's neck and kissed him deeply and longingly. Longing for love, the love that she had thought she had earned by being the perfect girlfriend, but had suddenly had it ripped away by the Army. Every time she pictured Matthew driving the new girl in his life home, walking her to her bedroom, or wherever, she kissed Timmy again. Kerry was a miserable drunk, and Matthew ran through her head non-stop. She took a few shots and talked to Timmy more, and she realized they didn't really have much in common, other than they both drank. She realized in the past that hadn't worked as the only means of communication, so he asked if she'd like to go to sleep a little early.

Kerry knew exactly what he meant, but she got up and followed him to the bedroom. Kerry didn't really want to, but after drinking so much, she was horny, and she knew deep in her heart that Matthew was going to do the same, or had already done so. And since that hurt, as least maybe she could have one night where she did the same. It was almost worse than she had imagined sex after Matthew would be; she wouldn't even let him finish; she simply got up, stood up really, because she had ended up on top somehow, and grabbed a blanket and left the room. Kerry went into the bathroom, cleaned herself up, took a few long drags of the joint hidden in there, and also washed her face while fighting tears the entire time. Not tears of regret, just tears of wanting. Wanting Matthew. Timmy could not please her anyway, and if he had been trying, he was failing miserably. Kerry went back in the room, after grabbing another beer, and he asked what was wrong. Kerry noticed that he had pulled his boxers on and thrown the condom away. She told him he was not doing much for her, because her mind was not with him. He looked pissed, with good reason, as Kerry had just told him he pretty much sucked, but he still tried touching her and getting her to change my mind. He was probably just trying to get himself a chance to redeem himself, as he rubbed her back and whispered how beautiful she was, and how he knew he was missing out on something great. Kerry silently agreed he was, but she had just sampled, and it was not good. Kerry straight out told him he would never be the true pleaser Matthew was, and she was and would always be in love with Matthew. He could touch her all he wanted, but he would never get with her, or even get the chance to get with her again. She chugged her beer and pulled the covers over her. He held her and rubbed her back and legs, trying to get her to change her mind, but Kerry just laid there and shivered. Kerry must have been a little too drunk, or maybe it was because she hadn't smoked in so long because of Matthew, but the window was shut, and Timmy said it was hot in the room, but Kerry still shivered like she was naked in a snowstorm. Timmy woke her up a few times, because he was scared she was having some kind of fit;

he really thought she was epileptic or something. She didn't know what was wrong, but it had nothing to do with the climate or anything. She just missed the warmth of love when she fell asleep in someone's arms. She felt nothing but contempt for Timmy. She could not believe she wasted the one night on someone who could not even please her. She knew she would never touch anyone again; she was going to wait for Matthew, and that was that. He was what she wanted, and until he told her that she would never again be his, or be with him, she wanted nothing to do with anyone. She still knew Matthew would still want her to at least go on dates and see if anyone interested her, but she could not. They were never going to be his equal. She already hated herself for letting herself get involved with her friends who had invited these guys in the first place. What if Matthew didn't do anything with anyone? In any case, she didn't volunteer her information about Timmy for fear he really wouldn't want her back. She really had only done what he'd asked, and sampled the field. And thrown it back, because it all disgusted her. She was so angry with herself, and she felt so nasty. What a stupid whore she decided she was.

57

Around the holidays, Matthew got leave. Kerry was dripping with excitement; he was going to fly in for Christmas, then Kerry was going to drive him back to Kentucky, and she would stay there until she had to return for school, which was only a few days. Maybe she could convince him it was a horrible idea to see other people. Unless he came home with someone, or told her he had someone waiting and she could just drop him off and go back to North Carolina. She hated herself for all this what-if shit running through her head. Why couldn't she just live in the moment and be happy he was coming home!? He would be there for their one-year anniversary, which Kerry still counted even though they had seen other people. After all, they were in different zip codes, right?

She met him at the airport, and he was still sexy as shit. She put aside in her mind that he had gone on a few dates, and that they hadn't panned out (Thank God), and she just enjoyed seeing him. Having him pick her up and hug her tighter than he ever had before. Maybe they had a chance yet for happiness and love. He had said that he was going to have to go to Afghanistan in January, so Kerry was taking advantage of these moments. Kerry never wanted him out of her sight. If she could drown him in love and attention, he would never want anybody else. Hopefully. Their anniversary was great, just time with each other. She bought a silky pink chemise to wear for him, and a flask with the date of their anniversary, and he cooked her a wonderful steak dinner for them to enjoy at her home. Kerry was just happy that he was in the same state as her for their anniversary, and that he wanted to see her and be there, and celebrate it. She'd have to drive him home the day after Christmas, so they had about six days. And she could only stay in Kentucky for about three. They did end up having a great vacation. It was like old times, and he was very attentive and very loving. All in all, it made Kerry very confused. Did he find anyone, and were they waiting for him to come home? Or was he not interested in anyone else anymore? For the most part of their vacation, Kerry ignored her obsession of what-ifs during his visit, and during the trip back down. Which was awesome, because she got to meet some of his guys. One said it was incredible to meet her, because Matthew talked her up and down. She blushed with pride. Even if he had seen other girls, he had still talked about Kerry. She met Jimbo, who turned out to be the craziest guy she had ever met, and Ben, whom Matthew was best friends with so far. He was awesome, and he spent most of their visit with Kerry and Matthew. They were an odd couple, always Kerry and Matthew, and Ben on his damn phone. He had three girls he called constantly. And he was a fun drunk. Crazy, and very talkative. Kerry stayed at Matthew's sisters' house with him. And at the time, both of his sisters lived there, in a little three-bedroom house, with both sisters, their boyfriends, and their children. Becky had two, Jenny had four of her own, and her boyfriend had two. The house was a zoo. But Matthew and Kerry huddled close, and stayed glued together the whole time. He didn't want her to leave when it was time, and Kerry honestly didn't want to go either. It almost would have been easier to leave had he wanted her to. But he wanted her to stay, and that was almost impossible for her to say she had to go.

Kerry was home about a week before her school had a little winter break. Matthew asked her to come down to see him before he left for Afghanistan. Kerry could not say no, because she knew she would not see him again for eight months, at least. The thought tore at her heart; eight months was a hell of a lot longer than boot camp, and Afghanistan was a hell of a lot more dangerous than Georgia was. So she packed up and drove over to Kentucky. He told her he had a present for her, but it didn't matter to her. The last present he gave her was a camelback that he had gotten for her in boot camp. It was a backpack that's sole purpose was to hold water while one walked or rode a bike. It was cool, but a weird gift. So she didn't care about the present, just the mere fact that he wanted her to come see him yet again before he left the country for war. They hung out with Ben again, pretty much picked him up off base, and he stayed with the two of them almost the whole time she was there. The first night, he had CQ, which is 24-hour duty at the desk, in case anybody needs a ride, or there is a call-up for everyone. That pissed Kerry off; she could only stay three days, and the first night, he was working. He said Kerry could have her gift the next day, because it was at his sisters' house. She brushed it off, because she hadn't driven nine and a half hours to get a gift. She was guessing it was lingerie anyway, because she assumed he'd want to see as much of her as possible before he left the country. He was leaving in a week. She hated that, and that the thought kept running through her mind. She couldn't stay the whole time, or she'd miss school. But a few days before she was to leave, she had called Angelica while he was at work and told her to please call her off of school, because she just couldn't leave him while he was still in the country. Angelica was very supportive, and told her to take her time, and to call her with updates. Jimbo, Ben, and his sister were all home the night before she was supposed to leave, and she told Matthew then that she had already arranged to stay a few more days. He hugged her like he was afraid he'd never see her again. God, it felt great. That safety she had yearned for, and was so afraid of losing. Becky had told her about some of the girls he had brought to her home, and she said she was grateful Kerry was there. She said she had wanted to kill a few. Those thoughts made Kerry feel nothing but relief. The first time she had met this sister, she had emphasized that Kerry was not going to get married anytime soon to Matthew. And Kerry felt that maybe Becky didn't like her, but she was welcoming Kerry into her already packed home, so Kerry felt at ease there, and welcomed into their world. Family. Kerry had always wanted sisters, and now she had his three that treated her like family. They all had a few beers, and the guys laughed and acted like fools, Kerry loving every minute of it. Then, they started talking about stuff they had done, and stuff they planned to do. Jimbo had just finished a story about something he had done, and Matthew got really loud and said, "I bet none of you has ever done this." He came over to where Kerry sat on the couch and got down on one knee. He looked Kerry right in the eyes and said, "Kerry, I love you, and I know we've been through a lot together, and it wasn't always easy, but I love you more every day, and will you marry me?"

Honestly, Kerry was so shocked, she just stared at him. The room had gone silent, so it hit Kerry that they all knew. They had been waiting for this, and Kerry had just been hanging out and having a good time. It felt like forever before she could actually speak, and it came out choked and shocked. "Of course."

He hugged her tightly, and she almost strangled him squeezing him so tight. She still could not believe what she had just heard. As he slid the engagement ring onto her right hand, Becky had been doing that thing where you cough and talk, trying to say "wrong hand, wrong hand." When they were done hugging, she yelled it. Everyone laughed, and Kerry had tears in her eyes. Becky had taken a picture of that precious moment, as Kerry's camera had been on the table. Kerry jumped up and hugged Jimbo and Ben, and kissed Matthew, and then they grabbed their cell phones. It was almost midnight, but they called all their friends, and Kerry's mom, who also knew, by the way. Kerry realized now why she had asked her to call with updates. Kerry felt like she was the only one who didn't know. When she sat down to think about it, everyone she called already knew it was going to happen, and Kerry was just letting them know she finally knew as well. Angelica knew a week before Kerry even went over to Kentucky, and she had told everyone she knew. Kerry couldn't believe she had kept that a secret. She was terrible with stuff like that. But Kerry kept twisting the ring, which was a bit too big, because Matthew had asked Angelica for her ring size, and she gave him the wrong one; she hadn't taken into account all the weight her daughter had lost, and she gave him her ring size from when she was fat. Kerry still couldn't believe it, though. She was *engaged*. She was going to *marry* him. He wasn't leaving her after all; he wanted her forever. It was like a dream. Kerry wanted to get bridal magazines right then, at midnight. Never in her life had she imagined getting married to anyone, much less in her twenties to the man that had given her more happiness in the short year she had known him than she had her entire life. They took a nice, hot bubble bath before they went to bed, and he asked her if she knew what she was getting herself into. He told her how difficult it was going to be married to an infantry soldier who would be overseas much of his career. Kerry just smiled at him, and told him how much it was worth waiting for him, whether it be fourteen weeks during boot camp, or three during jump school, or a year in Afghanistan. She told him she would make him happier than any other married man. He hugged her tightly in the tub amid the hot water and the steam, and said he knew she would. Kerry realized then that he had told her he loved her exactly a year ago. The thought made her smile. Now she had exactly five days to spend with her fiance before he left for Afghanistan. That thought did not damage her sleep, and she actually slept better than she had in months. In the arms of the man she was going to spend the rest of her life with.

The next few days were great, full of love and attention, and random looks fit for a queen or a supermodel. At the time, Kerry felt like both. She finally felt like the sexiest woman alive, and in Matthew's eyes, she had that recurrent thought that this was forever. She had never felt so much for someone. Never felt like it was the end of the world when he walked out of the room for work, and never felt like the sun was shining just on the two of them when he came home from work. Becky laughed because she told Kerry that the one night that his date had left a few weeks ago, he had sat down with her and said, "I want to marry Kerry." She had said, Thank God, and went to bed happy he would not bring any more creepy girls into her house. That meant more than anyone else's happiness for them. Becky had told Kerry not to marry him, and he wasn't ready, and now she had dramatically changed her opinion. Kerry had sisters. She had a new family. And she had his parents. His wonderful mother and his awesome father. Kerry finally could call him Dad, and it would be true. She had not only gained the best future husband the world had ever known, she had been welcomed into a truly wonderful family. Kerry could not wait to start planning.

58

The ride home from Kentucky wasn't so bad. Kerry cried for a minute, but then she realized he was coming home from Afghanistan, but he'd be without her while he was there, and she had to go prepare packages and letters, and get ready for their big day. She could not just sit around and be weepy like she had been during boot camp. Kerry was going to be a military wife, and she had to act as such. Stronger than any soldier, because she was the one to wait behind. To worry night and day what was going on, if he was sick, if he was sleeping okay, if there was danger near him. Kerry was now the helpless one who had to take care of business while he was off fighting for their freedom. Kerry felt the need to take care of his parents, although they seemed to not want it. They were happy for the two of them, but at the same time worried for their future. Kerry understood their worry, they were still very young, and had not been together for as long as most couples are when they marry, but they were sure of themselves. And nothing anyone said or did could change that. Kerry figured it would take a few days before Matthew was actually near a phone, because of his flight patterns to Afghanistan, so she went wedding dress shopping two days after she got back to North Carolina. And she ended up missing his first phone call. This gave her flashbacks to basic, but it turned out okay, so she figured he would call back soon. So she never left the house. Kerry had to wait until he bought calling cards, because he couldn't call her cell collect, and it would take weeks for a calling card to get to him if she sent it. Plus, she had to wait for an address to send to. And calling cards she sent, many, many times. She wanted to make sure if he was able to call, a missing calling card was not holding him back.

The first letter was direct, and to the point, mostly business, reassuring her that he was safe and well protected at his base. It wasn't as reassuring to her as she was sure he meant it to be, but her fiance was in a war zone, so how could anyone expect her to be calm and cool? She did do her best though, and didn't want anyone to think she was a wounded animal, waiting for something to happen to him. She was sure of him, confident in his training and dedication, and she was 100% sure he would come home soon, happy and healthy. She was already marking the calendar with the days he was giving her. In pencil, of course, because it could always change, but as of now, as of January, he would be home around August or September. They could get married before the year was out. Those thoughts made her heart race every time they ran through her head, and every time she looked at her left hand. It was crazy to see it wasn't a dream and that ring was still on her hand, sparkling beautifully with its meaning.

The first few letters ended in "love me," or "love your, hubby," and they made Kerry's heart melt. He even started writing Kerry Kilchern, instead of Kerry Riley after the first two letters. It had such a nice ring to it, and it was very cool to see it in writing. She still couldn't believe how lucky she had gotten. She had made it through a bad depression, and a few addictions, only to have the most wonderful man ever decide he wanted to be with her forever. They had taken time apart, and dated others, so they knew what they wanted, and they were going for it, deciding not to let it go. Kerry prayed to God every night not to take that away from her. Sometimes her prayers changed, and she merely prayed he would come home safe and sound, no matter whether he changed his mind or not, because she had learned during their time apart, that she could live without him if necessary (although she definitely didn't want to), but she realized that her love for him really just meant she wanted his happiness, whether it be with her or without her. And she thanked God for His gifts to her, and she made sure to reassure Him she would take good care of her husband.

I can't wait to marry you. I can't wait to see your beautiful face every morning for the rest of my life. I can't breath without you. I need you, baby, just remember how important you are to me. I also can't wait to make love to you. I want you so bad.

February

Kerry started working with Angelica at the magistrate's office, just until August, when she could start packing for Kentucky. She was kind of their slave, merely filing and answering phones, but she just figured until he came home, she could at least make some extra money for their future. Plus, since her mom worked there, she could keep her cell phone on her, and if it rang, he was more important than anything, and she could excuse herself to go outside to talk to him. She was also still in school. But she figured she wouldn't be able to finish before he got home, so this semester was to be her last, and she would start again in Kentucky. She truly dreaded that, as she hated school so badly. Especially this new college she had chosen. It was still close to home, and she didn't have to move out or anything, but it felt like high school. Had bells and everything, even in the evening and afternoon classes she had chosen so she could work at the office. And they docked students for missing days, so her grades were already slipping from missing the days to spend them with Matthew before he left. All in all, she didn't care.

59

At the end of the month, she came home from work as usual, and her mother was sitting on the couch crying instead of enjoying her day off. Kerry was hoping she was watching a sad movie, but it didn't appear that way, as the news was on. She told Kerry that Uncle Danny had died. At first Kerry couldn't speak or even think. Kerry just stood there, and then the explosion happened. She burst into tears, and, crying, she ran to her mother and let Angelica hold her as if she was an infant. That was the most horrible news she could have heard. Later, she hid in her room after her little fit with her mother, and she called a few people to cry on their shoulders, but it wasn't the same. She wanted Matthew here. Needed him here. And she couldn't have him. She wasn't even sure she should tell him what had happened. She definitely didn't want him to worry about her. Kerry had dealt with death before, and she was sure she could do it now. She had that repeating thought that she hadn't visited Uncle Danny for the holidays. She had been in Kentucky, and she hadn't seen him for their regular Christmas visit. She felt like she lost a father. A real one. It was an odd feeling, and, God forgive her, she wished it had been Calvin. She wouldn't have been upset, and her precious uncle would still be here. His funeral would be on a school day, so her grades would slip again, but she didn't care. The semester was almost over, and all she had to worry about was working with some woman who knew him and thought she knew him better than his own niece had. It was all Kerry could do not to punch her in the face every time she asked how Kerry was doing. Kerry didn't think it would be a good idea to attack a woman while working in a magistrate's office. Her dream of punching the woman was often with how many times she spoke of Danny, though, and Kerry secretly wondered where this she-male got her "girl manners." Didn't girls know when something was wrong, and politely avoid the subject, and try to talk about something else? Kerry was sure this insane woman had testosterone in her body somewhere.

Kerry kept thinking how all she had wanted was to have her 21st birthday with him. She wanted to have her first drinks with Angelica, Uncle Danny, and Aunt Andrea. They had always been there for her, and continued to be no matter how old she got. And she sincerely dreaded the funeral. The last one she had been to was horrible (not that there was one ever that she assumed would be easy), but now it was someone even closer to her.

The funeral *was* as awful as she had feared, and she sat in the room with his casket for almost an hour before anyone even spoke to her. She'd have preferred to sit there all night and cry in that room with him lying there so peacefully. She would never see him again, and she was trying to memorize his features, remember his laugh, and she wanted to remember how peaceful he looked one that day. Before the blood clot traveled to his heart, and he passed away. She had given brought him one white rose and one red rose, tied with a white ribbon. For peace and love, and tied together for a loving good-bye. She wrote him a note, gently folded in half, telling him she had never had a father like him before, and she would never forget all he had given her. She hadn't meant to anger anyone, but more people had opened the little card and read it, and those few words sent a firework explosion through that family and the entire funeral home. They were all asking Angelica questions, and Andrea questions. But Kerry wouldn't speak; she just smiled and walked away from everyone. Her biological father tried hugging her halfway through the night and asked how she was, but she shook him off and asked him, "How the hell do you think I am?" with much bitterness and pain in her voice. How she wanted Matthew to be there to carry her through the night. She just couldn't believe Uncle Danny was gone. He was the only one who was the father figure she had ached for while she was younger, and now he was gone. Forever. Kerry felt so lost, and she felt so much pain for her family. Andrea was lost, and his son was broken-hearted. Kerry hugged onto her older cousin as he seemed so much worse than Kerry was. He fought everyone off, but ended up letting Kerry hug him and hold him. Kerry needed that probably as badly as he did. One of her other cousins, who had moved to South Carolina years ago, took Kerry to him like an injured bird, and led her around all night, giving her new gossip, and staying in the smoking room with her, letting her cry and reminisce. He also protected her from some of the idiots who were trying to decipher her message on the card instead of remembering how great Danny had been. It appeared nobody in the family knew how Calvin had pretty much abandoned Kerry, and they all gave him looks of disapproval. He didn't seem to care. His wife was there, but not his children. It appalled Kerry that they didn't know how great their uncle was. And it infuriated her that they couldn't at least come to say goodbye. Kerry didn't even want to leave. To leave would be to accept that he was gone, and to never see his face again. During the eulogy, the minister pronounced her biological father's name wrong, and despite her inner angst, she had to withhold a snort of laughter. Uncle Danny would have laughed his ass off at that. The rest of the eulogy made her sit with the rest and mourn and cry the rest of the day. They all gathered at his old bar, and the bartender let Kerry have a drink. She chugged it because it was his last day on earth, and not below it, and it was for him, because her regret was that she could not share her 21st birthday with him. She had been waiting for it for years. Now she had to buck up, suck it up, and be a man, so to speak. She wanted to take care of her aunt and let her know how much everyone loved her and wanted to give her the world; all she had to do was ask. Kerry almost couldn't bear the pain, which she envisioned her aunt was bearing on a daily basis now.

60

March

Matthew's letters came pretty regularly, signed "your hubby," and they made Kerry feel a lot better, but it hurt not being able to tell him the turmoil going on in her head. She ended up deciding to wait to tell him about Uncle Danny. She didn't want him worrying about her while he was over there. He had enough on his plate.

> *I'll be wearing the three ribbons we earned over here already during this tour. I'm gonna be decorated like a Christmas tree. And I couldn't have done it without your love and support. I know a big part of you was hurt when I called from the MEPS station and told you I was going this last time. Look where we are now, our relationship has lasted through basic, jump school, and now a war. How many others can say that? Not many, maybe a handful. Marriages today aren't as strong as what we already have. I love you so much, baby, I'll be a great husband and father "down the road." No one will ever hurt you again. I can't express how much I love you. All I can say is I'm glad I went to the mall that day.*

Matthew got to call every once in awhile, and when he did, they usually got to talk for a long time. It was collect most of the time, but Kerry didn't care. She'd work overtime to pay the phone bill. It was just heavenly to hear his voice. Kerry stayed in close touch with his parents, and she usually visited his sister about once a week. She tried to keep pretty busy, and she always had a notebook, pen, envelopes, and stamps with her at all times. That way, whenever she had a free moment, she could write him how much she loved him, how much he meant to her, and how happy she was going to make him.

I love and miss you very much. As you're well aware. I never get sick of saying it either. I love you, Kerry Kilchern, and I don't care who knows it. Last night, I looked at the stars, and for every one I saw, I thought of a reason why I loved you. I was doin' fine until I ran out of stars.

Try not to worry, baby. You will be my wife and we'll be together forever. I'm very proud of you, baby. It's because you've been through a lot throughout your life and yet you have so much love to give. I'm just glad you give it to a bum like me. How could you not be smart and strong, you go to school and get good grades, go to work and deal with angry people all the time, and all the while thinking about me over here and worrying. Don't worry about me over here. I'm a well-trained killing machine that doesn't take any shit. They can't hurt me; no one can except you. But I have nothing to worry about there. I will be home and I will marry you, baby. I'm gonna keep on loving you, 'cause it's the only thing I wanna do.

April

The days didn't seem to be going any faster, and Kerry tried to fill her time, but it seemed like every five seconds he was running through her head. Dammit. Her birthday was coming up soon, though, so at least when she got upset or sad, she could go have a beer, legally. And, when he came home, they could go to the bar and tip back a few, and dance the night away. Besides, if Kerry was going to be around all those single soldiers, she would have to learn to be able to hold her liquor longer than them. Especially if the party was going to be at her house!

May

May was the month of her bridal shower, and a worse weather day could not have been chosen. Kerry stupidly wanted to have it outdoors, and believed since it was May, then it would be nice out. She could not have been more wrong. Belle was a God-send as usual, and she took care of everything Kerry couldn't even keep track of. She moved things, prepared the tables under the pavilions, and made sure all the food was prepared and set up properly. Despite the cold weather, everyone showed up in their heavy coats or sweatshirts and braved the chilly weather. Matthew was going to be shocked when he saw how much they received; it was a ton of stuff, nearly everything they would need in order to start their life in their new house. Kerry was totally shocked at the sheer amount of everything. Other than personal items, every single item for the bathroom, kitchen, and bedroom was already taken care of. Kerry wasn't going to need to buy anything, just get it ready when they moved down there. And since she had registered, and almost everyone looked at the register, it was everything she wanted. Her grandmother even took care of the fact that Kerry hated cooking by buying them a microwave. There were cards aplenty as well, some came through the mail, some were in a basket from the shower, and as Kerry opened them, friendly faces flashed through her mind as she read all of them. All the people through her life who had expressed any love for her were supporting her in the happiest time of her life. A few were missing addresses, so Kerry would have to search for them to send thank you cards, and since she had saved these until last, she didn't flinch at the one that had her name spelled wrong. A lot of relatives were spelling her name wrong. This card wasn't a bridal shower card, though, she realized as she pulled it out of the envelope. It had a strange set of flowers on the front, but no words. Inside, it had been sold as a blank card but someone with seemingly no distinct hand-writing had written just a few words: *You will always be just a mistake.*

August

Kerry barely made it through these months without going completely insane. Rare phone calls, letters speaking of only love and hope for the future, she could barely stand it if one day went by when he didn't call, email, or write to her. And that was a lot, because he didn't get his chance very often to do those things. They had him on missions and hiking up crazy huge mountains in the "wilds" of Afghanistan, and Kerry rarely saw what was going on, other than to watch the news, which was never a good idea. Kerry would sit with Matthew's mom, and they would concoct their own ideas of what he was doing or thinking or saying at that moment. They kept each other sane.

Kerry had a worrisome phone call when he was having his doubts as to whether they should get married or not, but Kerry more or less begged that he had to marry her. This hadn't been how she meant for the conversation to come across, but he was just worried that they were going to become an "old, married couple" immediately, and Kerry had no intentions of that happening, so she ended up pleading with him. Which was a horrible idea when she looked back now, because she had sworn SO many times that she would never beg or scheme in order to get someone to love her, or even like her. She had done that with Chase when she hadn't even wanted him really, and she decided afterwards that she wanted love for HER, only for HER. Not for pitying her, not for what they could gain from being with her, but only being happy and in love because of who she was in general. She knew it was so much to ask for, but she talked to him on the phone that day about it, and his reasoning was the same as every other "adult" that spoke to Kerry about him while he was gone. They were too young, didn't know what they were getting into, and didn't realize all the bills and stress they were about to endure. Didn't they know Kerry but at all? She had endured seeing Angelica live her life giving but never receiving the love from the man she dedicated a huge part of her life to, and Kerry had endured not having money to go buy whatever things were "in" that year in school. As a result of that, she had lived through taunts, ridicules, and harassment from everyone which started in elementary school up until a few months before she met Matthew. She had dated the frogs, and she knew when she had found the prince. She knew it wasn't lust, because she was living away from him, and she hurt mentally and physically from his absence. She wasn't pining after other men, or even looking for any, and she worried herself to the point where she had to take a garbage can to bed with her so she could throw up without having to get up and wake Angelica. She physically ached from the lack of his body being near hers, and there was nothing anyone could say to make it better. She had more than a few people tell her that they couldn't understand how she could make it without cheating on him. She simply couldn't even fathom the idea. Especially when some of these people asking her this were supposedly happily married! What could Kerry possibly gain from cheating? She wondered if the people who asked her that had ever really and truly "made love" because if they had, they wouldn't risk it for the world. They definitely wouldn't risk it because they had too much to drink and were horny. Kerry knew in her heart that even if she tried to cheat, she wouldn't be able to live with herself because she'd be so torn with guilt, and she also knew it wouldn't be worth it. Matthew knew how to please her, not just physically, but mentally at the same time. If it was a one-night stand, they weren't going to care about how Kerry "felt" afterwards, they'd be too busy looking for their clothes.

Other than the doubts that built up in her mind that Matthew wasn't truly ready for what he had proposed, literally, she blocked all negative thoughts with the planning of the wedding. If he did back out, Kerry would certainly be crushed, but at least the thought of the "happiest day of my life" could keep her busy. Kerry had already bought her dress, she had really enjoyed her bridal shower, and she was packing everything up in order to prepare to move to Kentucky. She never told him about the random, nameless card she received, and she never planned on doing so. She just knew that if he wasn't ready for her to make a life-changing move, she for sure was, and she was going to do it.

She had already decided that the packing part was definitely not a waste of time, because if he backed out of the wedding, Kerry was going to move anyway. Aunt Andrea had moved to Florida, and Kerry knew she would be welcome at her home with open arms.

61

September

The day was close at hand, and getting closer every day. Kerry drove over to Kentucky a week early in order to help Matthew's sister, Jenny, move into her house she was renting from the apartment she was currently in. Kerry was totally prepared for his arrival, and could barely stand to sit in Jenny's typically empty house daily and wait for everyone to get home from school or work so she could have company. Otherwise, she was wasting minutes on her cell phone or just channel-surfing. And she hated day-time TV. Kerry forced herself to stay in the house though, because she feared going out would entail spending money that they had been saving for their future. But, the day was set for his plane's arrival. Matthew's parents came down with Mel, and they stayed in a hotel nearby. Together, they were all ready to pick Matthew up.

Kerry stayed at Mom, Dad, and Mel's hotel room the day of his arrival so they could all ride together to pick him up. They had to get up around three a.m. to be there for his flight's arrival. Camera in hand, dressed as adorably and sexy as possible, yet shaking uncontrollably, Kerry followed Mom and Dad in Matthew's car. Kerry felt she could barely breathe as she waited for him, listening to the music from the band that was welcoming everyone's heroes home, and she nearly went insane at trying to pick the soldiers out from one another. It was obvious that they had all just had haircuts, and they were all wearing the same uniform, and carrying the same gear, the same cap covering half their faces, and Kerry drove herself crazy looking for Matthew while trying to act as though she knew exactly where he was. Then, Mel stated excitedly, "I see my brother!"

Kerry's eyes followed Mel's, and there HE was. Kerry had never seen anything more beautiful in her entire life. And he was trying to hide his joy and his smile, as he was supposed to be at attention. But, as soon as the officer's speech was over, and he let the guys loose, Mom ran to him. Kerry let the family hug him first, but when it was her turn, she squeezed him as hard as she could. Real, flesh and blood, all of him, all of her baby was home. He was here. It was a dream come true, literally. All she had wanted for the last eight long months was his safe return. Whether he returned to her or not, as long as he was coming home safe and alive would be sufficient. He was here, and he was hugging her as tightly as she was him. And he looked SO incredible. Kerry was positive that if the Army was good for anything not stressful, it was that uniform. Matthew ended up not being allowed to come with the family right away, he had to turn in his weapon and some other equipment, but Kerry slipped him the flask that she had brought for him. And she greeted Ben with open arms too; it was so awesome to see another familiar and friendly face who came home safe and sound. She felt sorrow for the people that didn't get to experience this, whether it be because they lost their loved one overseas, or because they didn't have anyone in the service at all. Kerry headed back to the hotel room with Mom and Dad, but Matthew called her about a half hour later and told her that she could wait with him there while he turned in his gear. Kerry immediately begged Dad for the van (she had let Ben borrow Matthew's car), and she raced back onto base to be with him. They actually snuck away to make love in the van (sorry, Dad), but it was so loving, Kerry had missed his strong arms, his loving kisses, and his warmth. It was far too much like she wasn't quite a whole person without him there with her.

They spent the evening at the hotel with his sisters (all three of them), Mom and Dad, and some of his buddies who were all so awesome. Kerry couldn't wait to be married and for her to be a true part of their Army experience. Kerry intended on making all the guys her friends/family. And, from the start, it seemed she had already fallen in love with them (as friends, of course). Matthew ended up drinking a bit (okay, a lot) too much for his first day home, though, and Kerry truly believed he had alcohol poisoning, but Mom and Dad angrily (with good reason) dropped the two of them off at their hotel, and since Ben still had their car, they were stuck there. Kerry wasn't even buzzed anymore after carrying Matthew up to the third floor of their cheap hotel with no elevator. His family was so angry with him that they just dropped the two of them off. Kerry wasn't upset with them over this though; for one thing, they had good reason, as he definitely shouldn't have drank this much, and for another reason, this gave her the opportunity to take care of him. She wanted to take care of him forever, so she might as well start now. After they got settled into the hotel room, he stayed in the bathroom for around two or three hours. His sisters, Becky and Jenny, came to see him, and he barely noticed they were there, other than to tell them to piss off. Which they actually found very amusing instead of getting angry. They were trying to get him to get up and go to dinner with the family. He could barely lift his head, so Kerry already knew they were in for the night, and she sat on the window ledge and smoked while watching the TV. Once he finally woke up, he took some headache medicine, and they took a bath to rid him of his pukey-smell, and just enjoyed having each other there.

Mom and Dad stayed for a few days, Matthew leading them to museums on base and off, and just spent family time with the sisters and the kids. After they were gone, Matthew and Kerry camped out on the floor in Jenny's living room, until they could find a house, and that wouldn't be possible until after they came back from leave…married.

After a few weeks in a house with seven children, they decided they needed a break, and they chose this nasty hotel because it was only $22 a night. It wasn't even worth that really, it was a mere trailer park with the trailers lined up and separated into two halves, which were the two rooms. The first night though, it wasn't bad, because they were only there about two hours, and then they were heading out to the bar to be with his sisters. It was "nickel night," and after the ten-dollar entrance fee, Kerry drank at least a few dollars worth of NICKEL beers. Then, when they left, Matthew and Kerry had to call a cab, because Becky thought they left already and ended up leaving without them. After they finally got to Becky's friend's apartment, where the car was, Matthew wanted to wait until he was sober enough to drive. Kerry tried to get some sleep because she was completely beyond wasted, but it didn't work, and she ended up in the bathroom and locked herself in, as she was in total embarrassment. And the girl who owned the apartment was NOT a girly-girl, or in Kerry's opinion, a clean girl, because she was out of toilet paper. What kind of girl ever lets herself run completely out of toilet paper, without even a tissue to fall back on? Ew. Anyway, Becky brought her a paper towel and a glass of water, and she sat on the floor in the bathroom and talked to Kerry for around a half an hour, or more, Kerry had no idea, because she barely even remembered what they talked about. What she did know, now, was that Liza, the girl whose apartment they were all at, flirted with Matthew constantly while Kerry was out of the room, and before Becky came to help Kerry, she told Matthew, "That girl is NOT going to trap you into marriage."

After the two girls talked, and Kerry ended up telling her everything, Becky changed her tune towards Kerry. Kerry told her every single worry, every single thing that happened while he was gone, everything about his family and hers, and all their friends, the lengths she had went to in order to please him and be with him…you know what, it had to have been more than a half hour. Anyway, she left the bathroom before Kerry did, as she wanted to clean herself up a bit (no mess, but she felt nasty), and Becky went up to Matthew, and she told him, "You better marry that girl; she lives her life for you."

After Kerry went out, Matthew was on the balcony alone, and he said he'd been thinking, but he didn't elaborate, but Kerry asked him if he was okay to drive, because she wanted to go back to their roach motel. Once they were there, Kerry didn't even remember if she kissed him goodnight, she just brushed her teeth and crashed into the pillow.

The next day, she slept on and off, throwing up some more, and generally being a sick nuisance. But, Matthew went to get them some food, and although Kerry tried eating some, she barely got any of it down. She tried, but the Sprite felt better than any of the food. They talked some, but mostly to pass the time, as the TV only got one channel. They were both lost in their own thoughts anyway, as Kerry was thinking of what to do when he stated that he wasn't ready to get married, and she honestly had no idea what he thought about in his silent reverie. Kerry knew he was concentrating deeply though, because he was silent most of the day, and she caught him glancing at her a few times, as if studying her. Once ready for checkout, though, they weren't at all upset about leaving that raunchy place, and they silently packed the car, and Kerry already yearned for the company of people who didn't have to decide how much they loved her.

After checking her voice messages, she saw that Mel had called and asked a question about her dress, so Kerry ended up having no choice but to bring up the wedding. But when she asked him if Mel should get the dress or not, he said, "If it fits, it's the right color, and she likes it, why shouldn't she?" Kerry assumed then that he regretted most of what he said the night before, and had made his decision that he was ready for marriage. Or given up on deciding, and was basing it on the promise he had already made. Kerry decided not to dig deeper into his emotions and his questionings, and let him be, and let the decision that they were getting married continue as it, pretending that the night before was a bad dream.

62

Once home, everything was wedding preparations. Kerry had a night with just her mother, and it was then that she asked her mother to be the one to give her away. Kerry couldn't see nobody doing it and her walking down the aisle alone, and Angelica was the only one who had been there for her no matter what had ever happened in her life. Angelica cried when she was asked, but was genuinely thrilled to be able to do this for her daughter. She had dramatically changed her life, and never spoke to Calvin, and never intended to again, and she was ready for her daughter to begin a married life. It meant her daughter already had the chance at happiness that Angelica had passed up by waiting around for so long. Kerry's girls, Belle, Candie, and Mel, had to go to different dress shops and pray that the colors matched the other two girls. Luckily, it all worked out marvelously. The dresses were all different in the way that they looked, but the colors were spot-on. So far, all the decorations and all the preparations were completed. Kerry was running around so much planning and getting everything they needed, that by the time all that was left was to get married came along, she was completely exhausted from everything. The certificates were made, and it was exciting to get their names on that paper, albeit a little awkward when it came time to put "father" information down, but Kerry didn't put much regarding him, and when the announcements were put in the paper he was not included. This was to be a happy time for her and Matthew, and *he* was not a part of it. The only people invited to the wedding from "his side" were her Aunt Andrea and her stepson.

The night before the wedding was wrought with tension. The decorating for the reception was after the rehearsal, which went perfectly, so the decorating was late in the evening, and everyone was getting tired. The decorating of the reception hall was stressful, and Kerry felt useless as their family and friends pretty much took over. Matthew was stressing over it as well, because they were both pretty much told to let them all handle it. He wasn't used to not having control, especially over something as important as his own reception, and he was getting rather irritated. Kerry was still fretting over the fact that she didn't even think the wedding was going to happen, so she wasn't bothering too much with the decorating. The stress that filled Matthew was radiating onto her, and it just reminded her of his nerves and the fact that she still thought he was still merely on the border of being ready. They had to sleep at each of their own parents' houses, because of the "not supposed to see the bride" rule, and that resulted in Kerry sleeping fitfully with Angelica.

Almost as soon as she went to sleep, she woke up bright and early around six am, not because she wanted to get up that early, but because it would take that long to get all of the girls' hair ready by the ten am wedding. Kerry wasn't excited, because she was still in denial that this was it. This was the day she had dreamed of, with the man she had dreamed of. Kerry and Angelica headed to Amanda's for her to do their hair, and Kerry prepared her make-up while waiting for the others to get their hair done first. Belle looked indescribably heavenly as her maid of honor, with her hair flowing and curling around her slim face, giving it a very dreamy look. Her lips matched Kerry's, lined with a subtle maroon lipstick, and they honestly looked like sisters, aside from the very different dresses. Everyone there took their preparation pictures, and Kerry cherished all of them. Actually, all the pictures turned out magnificent, and Kerry felt more beautiful than she ever had in her life. After she had her hair done, which was just above the shoulders, and Amanda had given it a very "princess" look, with long bangs sweeping along the side of her face, and her skin was flawless, except for a dimple every time she smiled. Her hair was curled a little at the bottom, and flowed ever so slightly in the slight breeze that swept across Kerry's perfect day. Her dress was sexy yet elegant. It was strapless and sleeveless, and the bodice had little sparkles embroidered onto it. The empire waistline was made even sexier by the corset Kerry had chosen, and her veil had teardrop gems hanging from it. Below the waistline, the skirt of the dress loosely flowed freely around her, just long enough to cover her "glass slippers," and it felt free and light on her, as if she were barely wearing anything at all. The glass slippers were her something old, as she had worn them in Mark's wedding with her elegant "best man" outfit. She had on a white and blue thong to hide her something blue, and the dress itself was her something new. Angelica came to her during all the preparations and handed her an anklet with two hearts intertwining each other for her something borrowed. Kerry believed she had covered all the "somethings" you're supposed to have, and she was more or less prepared to head to the church.

The parking lot was filling up quickly, and Kerry headed into the basement to get the flowers to all the girls and to wait impatiently, heart pounding into her brain, until ten am arrived. Then, Mel came down and asked that the ceremony be postponed (immediate panic arose), but it was because her cousin had flown in from Georgia, and she was on her way, but she would be twenty minutes late. It was fine with Kerry; if Matthew was important enough in her life that she would fly home from Georgia, then they could wait a few minutes. Although Kerry was already so nervous that she had to have someone in the room (her beloved and beautiful Belle kept her sane), while she paced back and forth, joking around to divert her attention to the upcoming ceremony. Honestly, the scariest part for her had to be preparing to walk down the aisle. That is, if no one came to her before she did that to tell her that it was being called off anyway. But, she hated having everyone's attention on her, and everyone was going to be staring, possibly criticizing, and their entire focus would be watching her walk down the aisle. Which seemed ridiculously long right now. She was relieved she couldn't find any flaws anyone else might notice, and that relieved her tension some. Once the time actually came, Kerry slowly followed her girls to stand in line. Her nerves were acting up, and she was getting really scared. Her little cousin, Kimmy, was in front of all the bridesmaids, walking with Bailey as the beautiful little flower girls. Mel, Candie, then Belle. The time came for Kerry. Each of her girls walked down the aisle to stand opposite of all the men who were already awaiting Kerry. Matthew, beside him was his best man and his best friend from the Army, Jim, and his brother-in-law, Jake. Beside them was Mark, as Kerry couldn't have him merely in the audience, and she had actually flirted with the idea of what he would look like as a bridesmaid, but decided against it. They were all wearing Afghani vests that Matthew had brought with him, except Jim, who matched Matthew with his dress greens. Their wedding was indeed unique, in its own simple way. When the time came and the music called for Kerry, she gripped her mother's hand desperately. Kerry took a deep breath and prepared herself mentally to head into adulthood without having a panic attack in the process. She took another deep breath, prepared her never-ending smile for the inevitable random pictures that would be taken, and stood beside her mother proudly. She didn't even look at Matthew while she headed down the aisle, for fear of what she would see. What did he think of her? Was he scared? Was he ready to run? As she glanced around the room, at the full chapel, she smiled as if there would be no tomorrow. Who knows, maybe there wouldn't be. Kerry felt rather confident as she marched down the aisle, her unsure future awaiting her at the end. She kissed her mom's cheek, as she put her hand into Matthew's. She finally glanced up at him then. His eyes showed his emotion. He was enjoying this as much as Kerry was supposed to be, and her heart eased and her mind relaxed. The rest of the ceremony went off without any problems, and when the time came, the pastor proudly announced his introduction of "Mr. and Mrs. Kilchern." It was surreal. Yet, it *was* real though, and Kerry was amazed at hearing how incredibly wonderful it sounded to hear her name. Her *new* name.

They headed outside, where more pictures were taken, and the bubbles Belle had passed out swam around their heads. Matthew looked like a type of God in his dress greens. After all the pictures at the church, then at an elegant garden of Belle's choice, the reception was close at hand. Belle's pictures were the most memorable and beautiful ones though, the lush gardens, the vibrant colors of the autumn flowers; everything was simply perfect for Kerry and Matthew's wedding day. She could hardly believe it. As they got into the backseat of their car, Jim was their chauffeur for the day, Matthew whispered to Kerry how beautiful she looked, and he said if he had any doubts, they were washed out of his mind the second he saw her walking towards him. Those words fulfilled Kerry's expectations of her wedding day. She suddenly and unexpectedly had everything she had dreamed of, everything she had prayed for.

63

Kerry's future was set; the reception was fantastic, with dancing, drinking, loving; everyone had a great time. The next steps to her future were in Kentucky, and she was as mentally prepared to be a military wife as she could be. She had kept that horrible card from her bridal shower, and it instilled in her a need to be brave, strong, and mentally better than whoever had written it. Once Kerry got to Kentucky, a whole new life would begin for her. A whole new story, and a whole new life of lessons in love and family.

Throughout her life, Kerry chose some of the easy routes, and some of the very wrong routes. This story is in no way supposed to make anyone believe that the answer to a problem is drinking, anger, drugs, pills, or anything even similar to that. This story is supposed to help anyone realize that speaking to someone they love, or a trusted professional, is the best route to take. They can make their own decisions after speaking to someone, and telling them the problems and issues going on in their life. If Kerry had spoken to her mother more and drank less, the problems she had later in life would have been non-existent. There is much more to this story, a marriage starts a new life, it's not the end of any life whatever. If there are mental problems, hidden issues, or anything traumatic, those things come out later in life, and that is why it's best to deal with them as they come along, not just go to a party and get drunk. Kerry was lucky enough to begin speaking with a therapist, because she was lucky enough to marry a man who actually cared that her past might affect their future. Anyone who thinks they might need to talk, merely has to find a phone number, a therapist, anyone, who will just listen. Advice is not always needed, and if someone isn't ready to actually speak with someone, a journal is the ultimate saviour. Write down what you think, what you believe, what you are afraid of. Writing is the ultimate release, and helps relieve most of the pressure that lies within your heart. Anyone in a similar situation, who believes their existence was a mistake as well, can learn to live as a mistake. Living as a mistake is a journey like no other, proving to yourself and to everyone around you that you are worthy of being happy, and, of course, being loved. God bless, and good dreams that come true to all of you.

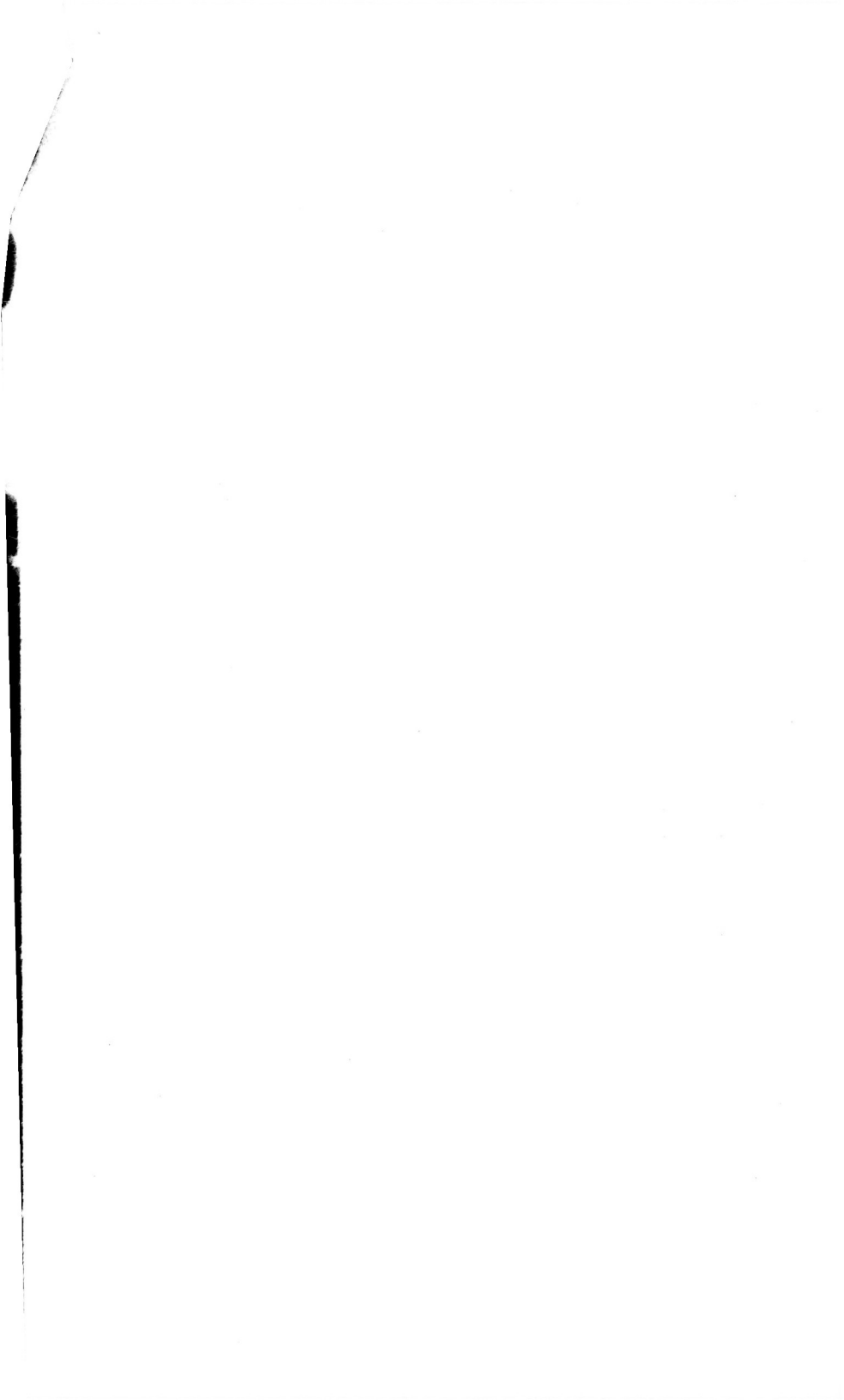